ALSO BY KATHARINE DAVIES
FROM CLIPPER LARGE PRINT

The Madness of Love

Hush, Little Baby

Katharine Davies

W F HOWES LTD

This large print edition published in 2008 by
W F Howes Ltd
Unit 4, Rearsby Business Park, Gaddesby Lane,
Rearsby, Leicester LE7 4YH

1 3 5 7 9 10 8 6 4 2

First published in the United Kingdom in 2006
by Chatto & Windus

A CIP catalogue record for this book is available
from the British Library

ISBN 978 1 40741 490 4

Typeset by Palimpsest Book Production Limited,
Grangemouth, Stirlingshire
Printed and bound in Great Britain
by MPG Books Ltd, Bodmin, Cornwall

FSC
Mixed Sources
Product group from well-managed
forests and other controlled sources

Cert no. SGS-COC-2953
www.fsc.org
© 1996 Forest Stewardship Council

CHAPTER 1

Spring was coming. Eira saw it in the way the wind ran through the plane tree outside her window. She watched the dark twigs catching at the air. Then she left for the museum. The front gardens of the houses trembled as they filled with light. She wanted his love to be like this light.

All day, Henry Lux talked about museum business and seemed to take no notice of the world outside. Henry Lux reminded her of the handsome mallards at the edge of the lake, when all the little globes of water ran off their backs like mercury. After the museum closed, Eira trailed home along avenues and groves where it was already night. She smelt a viburnum through the darkness. From an upstairs window she heard children's voices.

When she was a child, she saw her reflection once and she said to her mother, who was making the bed somewhere in the depths of the mirror, 'I have such a long neck, don't you think?' She pulled herself up tall for it to be admired.

'A long tongue is what you've got, Eira,' said

her mother, and it was true – she was always talking in those days. Now, there was Henry to talk to but she only listened and made small replies that anyone could have made. She didn't know if he imagined anything about her beyond the limits of these words.

The museum was in a park. It had once been a manor house and once a convent, the park being the old estate of both. Eira did not feel that she should ever have been someone who worked in a museum. She found herself thinking of the nuns. She looked out from the museum at the nuns' ghosts gathering, like pigeons, in the cedar trees, and she considered the lives of all the spinsters of the park, how they had measured out its history, pacing between the flowerbeds, thinking their red thoughts.

The museum had been the same since the day it opened. Its small collection was displayed in mahogany and glass cabinets. There were stuffed animals in a woodland tableau – a badger, a fox and a tawny owl. There was a smattering of coins, some crossed muskets, and hundreds of dead butterflies and moths in frames on the walls, and there were paintings of old men in stovepipe hats. Nothing you could touch. Many people who visited the museum thought that the most interesting thing was the beehive attached to an outside wall that had a glass window so that you could look inside. The bees would not stir until the summer months. Until last year, there had been a baby clinic on the first floor that had been there since the First World War. It had been an unusual place for a baby clinic, so people always said. Now, it was locked and silent; the grand staircase was no longer used, and no babies were ever carried past the seventeenth-century murals, or looked at the painted cherubs as if they were one of themselves.

At the heart of the park, a great and smelly stirring began among the waterfowl: Canada geese, coots, gulls, moorhens, ducks and swans – all their noisy languages blaring over the lake – and small birds burst from shrubs and flew across Eira's path. The oak trees waited fatly for their leaves on the empty grass plains that had once been the great forests of Middlesex. 'Once,' Henry said, 'the Virgin Queen hunted there.' But this was impossible to imagine. The snowdrops appeared, and after that the crocuses, and any snow that fell now died as it touched the ground. At last, the clocks sprang forward but the change of light only made Eira feel overexposed. Then the magnolias came out, creamy as brides. One day, she saw a man kiss a girl in the bandstand and a blackness came into her mind that would not go away.

Every morning, she walked down Sylvan Avenue towards the park. The net of branches above the wrought-iron gates began to blur with leaves. In her lunch hours she circuited the park, past the greening willows, the smell of green, the smell of the damp, black earth. The tips of the horse chestnut trees pushed through the moist air. Daffodils trumpeted their way around the circumference of the park at the foot of the railings. Mr Whippy chimed his chimes.

The park had everything you could wish for. As well as the museum, there was an aviary, a football pitch, a floodlit tennis court, a playground, a café that not only had ketchup holders in the shape of tomatoes but also served knickerbocker glories, a greenhouse with a banana tree inside, a herb garden, a sundial, a rose garden, a crazy golf course and a bowling green. When the sun shone, a man came to launch model boats onto the lake with a long wooden pole. When the wind blew, there were kites.

Eira knew her own spring had passed. She thought of herself as the faded moth, *Old Lady*, pinned through her thorax into her frame in the Long Gallery. *The Old Lady is one of the larger moths, attracted to the light in houses, especially in the country.* She had typed out these words. But, one day, she knew that Henry Lux would spread out the wings of her salt and pepper hair on a pillow and say, 'No. You were like a piece of light to me then, Eira.' She waited for this day. She prayed that the obstacle of Daisy Lux would be magically removed.

At night, she lay in her octagonal room at the top of a small tower that jutted out into Elmfield Crescent, telling herself a story of the sad death of her friend, Daisy Lux. The tower had a pointed roof with a spike at the tip, fairy-tale sharp. The glass in the window-panes was old and changed the shapes of things that came and went in the crescent. There were two other women who flapped about on the landing, whose smiles she brushed past on the stairs. Eira said to herself: 'We are the women of the bed-sit tower and we are out of tune with the spring.'

Every corner house had a tower. The houses in the streets that led away from the park were Edwardian flights of fancy with snow-fruit friezes under their eaves. Their top halves were white and their bottoms were red. They had flowery stained glass front doors with faded names above them that harked of the woodlands and fields that had not been so far away when they were built. Now, there was the North Circular Road, sirens, too much traffic and the taste of toxic air if you ventured away from the park's quiet streets with their ornamental cherry trees and ceanothus and darting birds.

One morning, Eira entered the park by the gardeners' gate, the first of the gates to be unlocked. There were whiffs of petrol from the lawnmowers and sweet, clean birdcalls in the air. Further in, the smell of night rain and dank lake water merged. Eira thought she was the first person to enter the park, but she could not have been the first. She was thinking how it is hard to know why we do certain things, that their import-ance is only later known, when she saw from a distance something at the top of the steps that led up to the museum door. She saw its whiteness against the dark stone. When she got nearer, she saw that it was a box.

It could have been a boxed doll, an anonymous donation to the small party of cracked and battered infants who lived in a glass case inside the museum. But it was not.

It was a baby.

A softly breathing baby, with skin the colour of tea, and sparse, black hair. Eira knelt down, her face, her ear, up close. The baby was fast asleep inside the box. It did not seem to be a newborn baby. It smelt of its own skin. A yellow blanket was tucked around it and there was a murky bottle of milk wedged at the foot of the box. Eira looked up and saw the wind move the green waters of the lake. She heard branches high above creak like spinsters' stays. She looked back at the sealed-up face in the box. It was her turn to unlock the museum. But here was a baby in a box, sleeping, out in the open. A sleeping baby. The lake water lapped between the rushes. A heron flew overhead, very near. Something else was being unlocked.

CHAPTER 2

I have made the window-seat in the junior library of Maldwyn Girls' College my own. I fit into it exactly – legs outstretched, back flat, like a bookend. All around me are walls of books. But it is not possible to read. My thoughts are trapped in the green heart of the woods at Priestmeadow.

I have pulled my grey socks over the eczema on my knees and tucked myself in with my skirt. I have paid no attention to beginning a new school. The only talent I have shown is for making myself invisible. I think of the summer behind me. I miss my mother. I miss my father. I wish that they had not gone to the University of the South Pacific in pursuit of the long-legged Fijian warbler and that they had not taken David away so that I will not see him for a whole term. I miss Maude. I think of her now, this afternoon, hunched over her kitchen table, or behind the issue desk in Priestmeadow Library, and of the long stalks of her handwriting in a letter she might be writing to me. I miss Uncle Huw and I miss Auntie Maggie. I miss Stella's barks and Midnight's miaows. And, even though Phyllis is right here in the sixth form of Maldwyn Girls' College, I miss her more than anyone because she is the one who will not speak to me.

If I cannot make her speak, I want her to look. If she looks at me, I will allow myself to become visible. I take out My Book from inside my vest. It is a pale green exercise book I stole from the stationery cupboard because I am stationery monitor and now it smells of my own body. On the outside I have written 'Eira Morgan: Her Book'. Inside, I have written one word: 'What?' I say this word over and over again until I sound like a bird twittering under the eaves.

The summer seems longer ago than it is. The summer was green and now the yellowness of autumn has come down over me. I want winter. I want darkness to hide in. I want dark mornings and dark evenings and the comfort of falling rain and to be doing my familiar puzzle of arctic animals at home on the floor of my bedroom in London. No one here knows what has happened. If you have a sister here, it doesn't mean she speaks to you. They don't know that Phyllis would have looked out for me. They don't know anything. In this school there is a brand new chapel with a royal blue carpet that gives you electric shocks. Sometimes, I go there and sit alone in a pew of honey-coloured wood and I look into a stained glass window in which nothing is very clear. I try to understand this picture. I stare at its jagged shapes.

I am sharp but I am also soft and blurred. I am screened from the world by my brown-framed specs, with the patch over the right eye, and by the thick, grey felt of my blazer and by my large, Hessian pump bag made by Auntie Maggie in her rather slapdash way. I look down from the junior library on the whirl of grey girls and out at the tiny, red-bibbed hockey team.

I hide my green book in the icehouse in the school grounds. I hide it in a hole in the trunk of a sycamore tree. It is there under my leotard when we are doing Modern Dance. I write another word, by torchlight: 'Why?' I haven't made any friends since I have come here. I don't want friends. When I arrived, I had to keep saying my name. I didn't want to. The teachers' faces said 'Oh, dear!' when they saw me in the register. My father says he chose my name because it means snow in Welsh. He didn't give a reason. I wonder why you would want to call someone snow?

'Perhaps because snow is beautiful from far away? Seen through a window balancing on the trees? Or when it is swirling in the air? Or when one flake lands on something dark, like a black velvet cloak?' These are the answers my mother would give. But I am not like snow. I am like someone who has been drawn in rough. Someone who you rub out before you start again and draw a proper person.

I didn't know about the junior library because

I hadn't been listening. I found out about it today when I was sitting on The Stump. The Stump is a thing of disgust. It is a thing avoided by the other girls because of the weird shelves of fungus sticking out of its sides. First, I watched three girls from my class squeal and scarper. Next, I crouched down and examined the fungus, which reminded me of marzipan. Then, by wedging my shoe-heel on a knot of bark, I hoisted myself up over it and onto the flat, dry top. The Stump is higher than it appears from grass level. It's like a pedestal for a statue. I stood up and pretended to be a statue. No one noticed. I sat down again. I looked at the empty part of the playing field where we are not allowed to go. The living trees are mainly oaks or sycamores and I wondered if this tree had been the only elm and had caught Dutch elm disease and if that is why it has died. I cracked off a strip of bark and I saw that the tree stump is, in fact, an insect sanctuary, a refuge for ugly things. I let a woodlouse run onto the tip of my little finger. In a space on the bright grass, the other girls who had squealed clutched each other and pointed back at The Stump, then they turned and galloped off, with their swish-swish hair, towards the high metal fence that protects the College from the railway line and keeps the Michaelmas daisies out of reach of picking. I saw how the light shone on their ponytails as they waved and pointed at the passengers of the one fifteen. I saw they were not pointing at me. They had not noticed me.

Three weeks of this new term at this new school, but the swallows still arrow through the air, like at Priestmeadow all summer. The leaves are only just dying and only just starting to come down.

All around me the other junior girls were screaming. Some had stripped down to their blouses, their long red ties flapping about at their necks. All around the edges of the netball courts, perched on narrow walls, the senior girls huddled and yakked and stretched their jumpers over their thumbs and over their big knees until they were allowed to go back inside. I knew, because Phyllis had told me once, that in the town, the sixth-formers were licking melted cinnamon butter off toast in Tatty's Tea Room or snogging Greenhill boys they met on the links and smoking their fags. She had said, 'Don't worry, Eira. I'll tell you what's what.' But she had not. I couldn't imagine Phyllis eating toast or kissing boys any more. I wondered if the black speck moving slowly along Green Edge that I could see through the crenellations of the school roof, and then not see, was her.

I hadn't noticed the on-duty teacher before. She was wearing a long blue tunic and had a pudding bowl of eerie black hair. I held my book in front of me and wished the sun could catch its cover and dazzle her and make her go away but there was no sun on our side of the playing field. She

11

came and stood before me like a medieval page, staring at my eye patch and the eczema on the knees of my crossed legs where my socks had slipped down with her big, weird eyes.

'Are you Eira Morgan?' she said.

'Yes,' I said, arming myself in my mind with Uncle Huw's walking stick.

'Sister of Phyllis?'

I nodded. My legs had gone liquidy. The teacher's arrival at The Stump could mean more awful things or it could mean that everything was over. I didn't want it to mean nothing, that things would just go on.

'Well,' said the teacher, Welshly, 'I would never have guessed!' I saw the teacher noticing other ways in which I was different from Phyllis. We looked at the playing girls. Things were just going on. The teacher's eye settled on my book, *The Traveller in Time*. It is the only book I have brought with me to Maldwyn Girls' College. It's because Maude gave it to me. I pressed it down in my lap. Uncle Huw always said, 'You are never alone with a book.' But he didn't mean like this.

'Have you been to the junior library? It is where we go to read,' said the teacher.

I looked down at her face. It looked as though she had swept her powder puff along the ledge in front of the blackboard.

'No. It's all right. Thank you so much.' I pretended to read so she would go, but she kept on standing there, watching me, until a group of

12

second years bore her away to a girl who had fallen flat on her face because they had pushed her over. If you are the ugly little sister of Phyllis Morgan, and you have to wear a patch over one of your eyes, she meant. It is somewhere you can go to hide your funny skin.

The lunch hour had thirty-five minutes left and the trio was cantering back from the railway line so I got down from The Stump and cut through the high din of the playground. Two girls clapping their hands together, and singing *Under the Brambles*, locked eyes as I passed. I gave them my one-eyed stare but I didn't care about them because I only cared about Phyllis.

At the corner of the quad, there was a man in a brown overall, sweeping, so I asked him where the junior library was. He is the only man I have seen here. He cocked his eyebrow in the direction of the north tower. The staircase of the north tower is made of slippery black wood. Halfway up the stairs, I hesitated. A door bashed open and the games mistress ricocheted down the stairs. Behind her there was laughter. Lipsticked mouths. Smoke. Chalky voices. On the next level is another door with a tiny brass plaque on it saying North Library, not Junior Library – just to confuse people, I suppose. My first thought when I opened the door, the floor falling away from me so sharply, and the floorboards being so black and uneven, was that it is more like the inside of a ship, even though the only kind of ship I have been on is a ferry.

It smells interesting here, sweet and warm, as if the books are made of biscuits. There is no librarian. There is a red exercise book on the table with a short pencil hanging from it by a string.

I slid over to the middle of the room. I was alone for the first time in three weeks, except for my visits to the chapel. You can never tell if someone has come in behind you when you are in the chapel. If Phyllis had been speaking to me, she would have told me you can come here to be by yourself if you are in the lower school. I listened to the floorboards creaking under my shoes. I turned round and round and looked at the rows of books and saw the stepladder you have to climb to reach them. It is only a small room, not like Priestmeadow Library, with its children's picture books and large-print hardbacks and the spinning rack of Mills and Boons. There are two tall windows with wavy glass in the panes. Through the glass is autumn and girls playing. In each window there is a window-seat with dark red cushions. I am in the left hand one, furthest from the desk, above a section marked 'Reference'.

The chapel clock is pinging in the distance. An old, crumpled teacher pokes her head round the door and says, 'Come along, girlie!' and I look down on the grey girls milling below because this is a refuge from their shouting and I don't want to leave it. There has been a rhythm in my head all day, like tom-tom beats, and only now can I hear that it has words: 'Phy-llis is shrink-ing, Phy-llis is

14

shrink-ing, Phy-llis is shrink-ing . . .'. I think of Priestmeadow, heavily green and full of whispering leaves as it had been in the summer; of the damp, cold smell of the stone bridge; of the Jenkins's dairy; of Uncle Huw's smoky-leathery study and the cool covered yard. Stella whisking about. Auntie Maggie prising open a tin of Gumption. It will all be going on as usual but with some of us missing.

Last week, Janet McTavish said, 'Ayrar, you talk in your sleep.'

'Nothing that people say in their sleep is ever true,' I told her.

'That's not what I've heard,' said Janet, 'but you mutter and I can't work out what you're saying, anyway.'

Since then, my nights have been wakeful, dreamless, the dreams I might have dreamed shoved down, like the peelings at the bottom of Auntie Maggie's compost heap. In lessons I am tired. Sometimes, I have a feeling that I have risen up to one of the beams in the rafters. The only person who could tell me what to do is Maude. A vision of Maude comes to me, sitting on a stump, knitting one of her foolishly long-armed jumpers.

'Set it down,' says Maude. At first, this makes no sense. It feels as though I am being asked to drop a sack of coal.

'In pen and ink,' says Maude. *'In autumn, when the leaves are brown, take pen and ink and write it down'*. The words of Humpty Dumpty.

15

Janet has a question for me as we get out our books for Latin: 'Is Phyllis Morgan your sister?'

'Salvete, puellae!' says Miss Fowles.

'No. Salve, magistra!' I say. 'We are estranged.' I don't think Janet knows what estranged means.

The Latin teacher writes some lists of verbs on the board in her big, babyish writing. Janet is watching me with her detective expression. 'What is your patch for?' she asks politely. 'Are you blained in one eye?

'This eye,' I say, pointing to my un-patched left eye, 'is lazy.'

'Oh,' says Janet. She sounds disappointed. 'But she is your sister. I know that for a fact.'

I stare at the board at the words we are supposed to copy. Miss Fowles is slumped against the radiator. Amo, amas, amat. I love. You love. He, she or it loves. He loved her. He loved her not. My book, with its 'what' and 'why', is lying against my chest. Everyone is just doing this copying. The windows, so high in the wall, are merely air vents. No one could possibly see out of them anything except sky. A Red Admiral butterfly has got trapped on the wrong side of the glass, beyond my power to save. When this is over, there will be French and Prep and some sort of nasty supper like steak and kidney pie followed by semolina, and on and on. Phyllis is probably in the art room, painting one of her red paintings à la Munch. I hope Miss Finch has let them out into the grounds to draw the trees like she did last year and that

Phyllis will still be able to find it in her heart to draw a tree. Perhaps a red tree, like a maple? A thing so lovely. I watch my writing form and now I want to be writing in my book and now I know what to write but I can't because I am copying out these dead words.

CHAPTER 3

Eira stepped forward. Quick. Shaking. The natural thing would have been to take the baby inside the museum, from light to dark, from present to past. To take it in, like in a story. But Eira found that she could not do this. The pigeons shifted their positions in the trees.

'Keep you safe,' she said.

She checked the bushes again for spying eyes. She didn't wait for anyone else. Not for whoever had left this poor baby. Not for Henry Lux, who that morning had taken Daisy Lux to the hospital. Not for the park keeper or any of his team. She lifted the baby out of the box, with its blanket still around it, and placed it in the cradle of her handbag with more tenderness than she had ever had the chance to do anything. She fastened the straps loosely so she could still see inside, the baby's face a rose of sleep – a tea rose! She decided that the baby was a girl. She waited to see if the baby girl would go on sleeping. Some subtle expressions flitted across the baby's face but she went on sleeping. Eira lifted the bagged baby close to her chest and held her tight. Grass blurred, birds scattered, there was the swish of traffic, a zebra crossing, the beeping of the green man. Then she was away from the park and onto the pavement of Sylvan Avenue, her eyes pinned on her tower through the trees. Her legs felt light but her heart was strong and singing. There was no crying. The baby kept on sleeping, sleeping, sleeping, all the way down Sylvan Avenue. Keys. Dark stairs. Shut door without a sound. Take out the baby, all in her yellow blanket, feeling the weight of her. Safe.

'Now,' said Eira.

She put the baby on the bed near the pillow end, flat, and this made the baby's eyes open and the baby moved inside the blanket and part of the blanket fell away from the baby's bare body and her hands opened and closed, exploring. The baby was silent, breathing, clad only in her nappy. Eira touched the baby's cheek with the back of her finger and felt the unearthly softness of the baby. She noticed the curled petals of the baby's ears. She looked into the baby's round, dark brown eyes and the baby looked calmly back into Eira's and seemed to see beyond her specs and to know that she was human.

'Hello,' Eira whispered. 'Hello.'

She drew the curtains and sat down on the other side of the bed. In the gloom she heard traffic and people on the pavement and buggy wheels – other babies being transferred from A to B. Crying. The baby's curled ears also heard these things and she started crying too, a cry that grew louder and louder and louder until it moved something inside Eira that she had been pretending wasn't there. She attempted to rewrap the blanket around the baby's body but the baby did not want this. The baby was panicking. The baby wanted to be picked up. Eira was panicking. At last, she obeyed the baby and the baby stopped crying. She reached out towards Eira's left breast and Eira intercepted the baby's tentacle fingers and shook them lightly up and down. The baby made a sucking noise. Eira leaned over to get the bottle of milk and smelt again the smell of skin and spice, as she steered the rubber teat towards the baby. The baby locked her mouth over it watchfully. Eira had seen other people feeding babies. She lifted up the bottom of the bottle. She went over to the wardrobe mirror and looked at herself. She imagined this were her own baby and she swayed her from side to side and sang, 'Hush, Little Baby'. She stopped singing. The baby had loosened her mouth-hold on the bottle and was quiet, absorbing everything. They looked at each other for a long time and the difference in their ages was very stark. Eira picked up her keys. The baby was mesmerised by the keys.

Eira wished that Jack could see her with the baby. The baby was solid, a weight in her arms. A good weight. The baby was good. And the baby wanted to be there.

'You are a remarkably good baby,' she said to

the baby, kissing her warm scalp, and the baby looked faintly amused and nothing happened for a long time. Eira could only think of Jack. And how, if he saw her like this, everything that had once seemed impossible would become possible. More time passed. Eira stared into the shadows of the octagonal room and the room turned into a maternity ward and the shadows turned into Jack sitting, as she had always pictured him sitting, holding her hand tightly, and looking at her as she had always imagined he would look, one day, when their baby was born. Then Phyllis was there in another room with moth-eaten curtains – a long, long time before she met Jack – telling her she was a stupid idiot.

Down the avenue she went with her baby cargo, out in the open this time, in her arms, with the yellow blanket. The baby started crying. In the queue at the doctor's, Eira cried as well. The faces in the waiting room turned towards them, like leaves flipped by the wind, and then away.

'I found her,' she said to the receptionist. She lifted up the baby, carefully, but now the baby screamed and writhed as if she were about to die. The receptionist's hands paused on her keyboard.

'What is your National Health number?' she said.

Eira turned around, and as she did so she saw herself running back to her tower and hiding with the baby and looking after her, feeding her formula milk in secret for days and days until the days became months and years and she became the baby's mother. And, at the same time, she saw that this would be the act of a stupid idiot. There was a smiling woman in an orange sari with arms like the handles of a vase. Eira put the baby on the silky lap and the woman's arms linked themselves around the baby to stop her sliding off.

Eira ran out of the surgery. She ran home and got into bed with all her clothes still on, with her coat still on, and her shoes, and curled herself up like the baby's ear. There was a school party arriving at the museum at ten. She thought of them all waiting outside the museum. She did not care.

She imagined the baby's real mother hurtling over the wide green grass, looking everywhere, changing her mind, finding a box of air. Eira got up. She ran past the surgery, back to the park, now full of other people who could have found the baby. She wished one of them had found the baby instead of her. The box was still on the step, an ignored empty box of nothing. The children had walked from the primary school at the other side of the park in a crocodile. One of them kicked the box. They didn't notice that Eira was panting for breath, that she was only just opening the museum. They had come to look at the butterflies. The children had silky heads and big eyes and they flocked around in the half-dark and filled in their worksheets noisily. The children laughed at the stuffed fox with a blackbird in its mouth, at the black and white stripes of the snarling badger killed in the countryside of long ago, at the shiny guns and sparky swords and at the iridescent butterflies and the beige moths stabbed into their frames in the Long Gallery. What was happening to the baby now? Eira kept a look out for someone who might be the baby's mother. She felt hot and burning and then suddenly cold. She thought of going back to the surgery. But no one came and she didn't go back. The children were loud and brash at the same time as being delicate, flighty and perfect. They were loose and free and Eira knew this was something she wanted for herself. The teacher collected the flutter of worksheets and the children ran out onto the grass. When Henry came back from the hospital, he said that Daisy was being kept in for observation. Then he brought the white box inside and flattened it with the heel of his hand.

CHAPTER 4

The next day, Saturday, was Eira's day off and she caught the bus to Muswell Hill. The sky was full of dark grey cloud but, as she walked towards her parents' house, the sun came out and the forsythia burned bright in garden after garden. A robin flew between the bushes, never letting her get too close. She had only once touched a bird. When she was a child, she had wrested a fledgling blackbird from the jaws of Midnight. She had cupped the jittery body in her hands and, when she saw it could not fly, she had made it a nest of grass in a shoebox and provided it with water and worms. She had watched over it, and it had looked back at her with its round, black eyes and scuffled in the box. But on the next day, it was dead.

She opened the door of the spare bedroom to the recorded songs of Fijian birds. Her father was cooped up doing his bird paintings, listening to the voices of his subjects as he worked.

'Hello, Dad.'

Whoops and whistles. She wanted him to hold her in his arms while she told him about the baby in the park.

'Hello.' He blinked at her and turned back to the easel. She couldn't see what kind of bird he was painting. His speckle-backed hand dipped and swirled his brush into paint and patted it against the canvas. She stepped further into his forest of books and paper and pots and jars of paintbrushes; there were piles of bird skeletons and there were tropical tail feathers in vases. The stuffed shrike was still suspended from the ceiling in its endless flight. Outside was all sky, a sky that suggested the coming of rain. Seagulls crossed the window in small flocks. But these were not her father's birds. They were nothing to him and Eira knew he never noticed them, not even when the sun made them look silver or pink at dawn and sunset because their feathers were white. Her father painted the orange dove of Fiji, the velvet dove, the Pacific golden plover, the spotted fantail. He painted them still, sitting on branches, with whiteness behind them, which was not white sky, but just whiteness.

'Hang on,' he said. If you can come to me now, she thought, it will be all right. But he did not come. He carried on painting. He let himself be watched, his elbows winging out, his own patchy, multi-coloured feathers dabbed on where he had wiped his brush on his painting shirt. He painted his birds from photographs, from memory and from the knowledge that was stored inside his brain from his scientist years. He was surrounded by birds in progress, hung on the walls, held

25

captive by the edges of their canvases. Not one of them was finished; in each an eye was left blank, or a wing was missing; some were footless and some had no beaks. Eira did not know why he should do this but they seemed significant, these gaps. He looked at her between birds, between brushstrokes, his eyes very dark and clear and he was not, in that look, her father at all. He put down his brush, wiped his hands on a rag and took off his painting shirt.

'Well, well,' he said, pecking her cheek. She put her arm through his and they stood in the middle of the room with the unfinished birds and their recorded songs all around them. 'If only they could paint themselves!' he said, as if his paintings were a necessity, a task that had to be done, come what may. The front door banged shut.

'Ha!'

There were sounds of her mother in the kitchen, sighing, getting things out of the cupboards for lunch and the radio coming on to the closing head-lines of the news. Eira left him washing his hands and went halfway down the stairs to a small landing that looked onto the back garden. There was a china milkmaid on the window ledge that Auntie Maggie had given to Phyllis the last summer at Priestmeadow. It was just a girl. A cold, white, little china girl in an old-fashioned dress. Eira picked her up and pressed her against her cheek, peering down at the gardens far below – to the left, brambles, to the right, a rectangle of green with cherry blossom out and a climbing frame, and, in the middle, her parents' garden engulfed by its big grey patio. Eira's stomach clenched at the thought of telling her mother about the baby in the park. She could not say the word 'baby' now without wanting to cry. She watched some children playing on the climbing frame, two girls; the smaller one was copying everything the bigger girl did. Her mother walked out to the edge of the patio and scattered some crusts for the birds. Blanche appeared in the border getting ready to pounce, unaware of her obvious whiteness, the reason she never caught anything.

Her mother was waiting for her by the newel post at the bottom of the stairs. She seemed to be getting flimsier, shakier with every visit. She had the radio on the lunch table and it was *Brain of Britain*. '*Shall I compare thee to a summer's day?*' '*Thou art more lovely and more temperate,*' said her father coming down the stairs. Kathmandu. 25. Einstein. Potassium permanganate. Hummingbird. The rain applauded on the roof of the conservatory, then, after the darkness of the rain, the sun came out and flashed on their cutlery as they ate and on the rims of their wineglasses. They stared away from one another, away from thoughts of Phyllis. Eira tried to formulate a sentence in her mind that would not make her cry, failed and stayed silent.

Afterwards, her father went back to his painting

and she and her mother sat in the conservatory. There was a rainbow. Blanche came and sat on her mother's lap.

'She never lets me touch her,' said Eira.

The sun shone between the pickle-jars still left on the table. Blanche closed her eyes, safe from the far thunder. Her mother had started doing tapestry again; a telltale frame stuck out of a workbag by the side of her chair.

Eira met her mother's eyes. 'I'm perfectly all right,' her mother said, taking up the tapestry crossly, a butterfly on the wing. She pulled out her tapestry wool, more and more spooling out, ravelling and unravelling as she talked about the colour scheme, about the secrets of how tapestry is done. Eira went back upstairs and stood behind her father, watching him layering on the feathers of a velvet dove. It looked as though, if you could dive your hands into the picture, you could scoop him out and hold him, and feel his beating heart.

'It's therapeutic,' said her father.

One Christmas, when she was six, they had given her a brown stuffed cat with fur the texture of a sheep's wool and a springy tail like a kangaroo's. Its eyes and ears had been sewn on wonky and Phyllis and David had laughed at it. But Auntie Maggie said it was made by a blind man in Priestmeadow so Eira had christened him Cocoa Handiwork and held him against her chest every night.

'I can't stay long,' Eira said.

They both came and said goodbye on the doorstep. Her father touched her cheek with the edge of his lips. Her mother's hands felt cold and stiff despite the exercise of stitching. As Eira's steps took her away from them, she thought of theirs retracing their well-worn tracks – her father's back to his easel and her mother going back to her tapestry and her chair in the conservatory, gathering the dead leaves from the geraniums as she went, winding up her wool. There would be the voices of the afternoon play downstairs and the voices of the birds high above.

She walked further and further away from the house where she and Phyllis and David had grown up and she kept walking along wet streets until she got to Alexandra Palace. She stopped by the balustrade in front of it and looked out at London so no one could see her face. All she could think about now was that last summer at Priestmeadow. The summer when she was ten and Phyllis was seventeen. She had never wanted to think about it again.

CHAPTER 5

'It wasn't always like this,' I say to Janet McTavish, in my head, after lights-out.

Only three months ago, late one evening in July, Uncle Huw was driving us through Priestmeadow and out the other side and down the bumpy lane that leads to their house, and saying 'A-bloody-men' as he switched off the engine. I could hear David's breathing at my side, the crick-cracking of the car cooling down, a singing in my ears. I was happy to be there. I was so happy that I thought everyone else was too.

'David,' I said, 'wake up.' David had been sick at the side of the road in Worcester, Bromsgrove and Kidderminster. He didn't wake up so I left him.

'Look at the moon!' Uncle Huw said as we got out of the car. '*Like a ghostly galleon tossed upon cloudy seas*! Wouldn't you say?' At first, I couldn't say but then I saw that the moon could look like a big sail billowing in the wind and the clouds underneath could be like waves if you wanted them to be. A phantom ship. I took a big breath of air because I had been fighting my own secret battle not to be sick and now it was over.

'That's right! Breathe the Priestmeadow air. Now you're away from The Smoke.'

I could see three figures at the open front door: Auntie Maggie, Phyllis, and a tall man who I knew must be their famous lodger, Edward Furnace. They waited for us to come towards them, their faces all dark because the orange light from the house was behind them. The house seemed to be a black cage filled with golden air and they were black, inquisitive birds looking out. The air outside was musky, the smell of night blowing out of the sky and across the garden. Someone must have heard the car as we swung through the gate. It would probably have been Phyllis, kneeling up on her bed looking out of the window at her own reflection or at nothing in particular as she was always doing at home, 'thinking' as she liked to say, to annoy. Auntie Maggie would not have heard the car. She would have been shut away in the kitchen with Midnight on her lap, darning her big jagged stitches onto socks and boiling giblets to the tune of her jaunty radio music. I didn't know where Edward might have been because I didn't know his habits then. Perhaps he had been talking to Auntie Maggie, sitting on the high, red stool where David or I usually sat. Perhaps it was Stella who heard us, the black triangle of her ear flipping open like a magic door. Uncle Huw staggered across the weedy tarmac in front of me, and Stella shot forward and lassoed him into the house with her

31

invisible rope of dog-love. Auntie Maggie darted into the darkness and scooped David off the back seat into her arms. As they came up behind me, he woke up at last and said, 'Hello, Auntie Maggie. Actually, I can walk, you know.' So she put him down and she pulled me against her overall on the other side. 'Child,' was what she said to me. Phyllis and Edward were standing awkwardly together in the porch.

'Shall I help with the cases?' Edward asked, but no one answered and I went to Phyllis and she put her arms round me.

'Hello,' she whispered. I looked into the mystery of her mysterious face.

'Are you better now?' I said, not having seen her for months, feeling in the dark for flesh on her bones.

'Much.'

We went in and the house smelt of their house – coaly, dusty, yet polishy, with hints of roast-dinners-past trapped in corners. The grandfather clock struck ten. I adjusted my eyes to the pattern of the rug in the hall and followed it into the snug. Stella slunk along by my side and my palm flowed along the soft, black waves of her fur. Uncle Huw was already in his brown leather chair, doing his silent might-be-a-heart-attack laugh, before his head nodded down onto his chest and he was asleep. Edward bounded in and then back to the doorway again because there weren't enough seats.

'Tea?' said Auntie Maggie, and David and I had milk in cups and saucers.

When we got up to go to bed, Edward collapsed into our gap, as if he were one of the family, and Phyllis got up, as if he were a lever ejecting her from the sofa, and went out to the kitchen.

The dried seedpods of honesty on the landing window-sill quivered and shook in their vase as we passed, a hundred more moons. Auntie Maggie snapped on the light in our room and I breathed in the smell of dusty toys. There was the bunk bed for David and me and there was Phyllis's bed under the window with its pink shiny counter-pane. David had already climbed the ladder to the top bunk and I was too tired to argue so I just got into the bottom one. My pillow felt cool. It had an embroidered blue boat on it, meant for David, like the one Uncle Huw saw in the sky. Auntie Maggie kissed me and I must have fallen straight to sleep. Later, I heard Phyllis coming in, brushing her teeth quietly in the dark, spitting into the basin, and I remembered I had forgotten to brush mine. During the night, I heard David wheezing and coughing in his sleep, like a little old man.

I was awake first. The garden was full of birds and I thought of Mum and Dad in Fiji scouring the undergrowth for their long-legged warbler. I put on my specs. The sun was shining through the holes that the moths had eaten in the curtain-flowers. The toys were all tucked away: the dressing-up clothes in the drawers of the dressing table, the farm – with its silver-foil duck pond, lead animals, hedges and trees and pretty milkmaids – in boxes under the bed. In the wardrobe were Noah's Ark with all the pairs of wooden animals, and David's set of metal trains. I could see my small red case in the middle of the floor. I tiptoed over to it, unzipped it very quietly and felt around for my toothbrush. I crept over to the basin and slowly ran the tap, but not so slowly as to make the pipes bang and wake the others. The water tasted of pipes and stones and moss. Under her pink counterpane, beneath the black storm of her hair, Phyllis was still asleep. I looked across at the top bunk and saw David was rubbing his eyes.

'Tonight is my turn on the top,' I whispered on my way out.

Auntie Maggie's door was ajar. I could see a glimpse of her dressing table with its temptation of glass bottles and her special, ivory-backed brush that she uses to give her hair a hundred brush-strokes every night and every morning before she does her plaits. Her window was open wide and the sound of birds was even louder. I knew she'd be downstairs as she always is when you wake up and when you go down she is there, cleaning out the grate, laying sticks in the fire, getting buckets of coal from the covered yard, or, in the summer, bashing dust from cushions and beating rugs. Last of all, she gets the vacuum cleaner from the cupboard under the stairs and charges round like the Jabberwock. Then there is bacon to be fried. Eggs to be scrambled. Bread to be toasted. Pots of tea to be brewed. The front door was wide open and a chain of Stella's wet paw prints lay across the hall like an invitation out.

'Aren't you dressed, child? Where's Uncle Huw?' Auntie Maggie said.

'Doing his ablutions,' I told her. Stella had found his pyjamas on his bed and brought them down for Auntie Maggie and she bent down and wrestled them from Stella's slobbery mouth. I ran upstairs and David was just coming out of the bedroom already dressed.

'I'm going outside before I've even had my breakfast!' he said, as if this was the most shocking thing that had ever been done in the world.

In the garden David and I were hoping to see a woodpecker, a hedgehog or a rabbit, but all we saw were lots of wood pigeons. The grass was wet and cobwebby. We ran under the nets of the raspberry patch, swung on the rusty swing in the spinney, found the coalhole, found snails, little black ones with yellow shells. Then there was a tapping on the dining room window. It was Uncle Huw holding his hands in prayer and casting his eyes up to heaven. It was Sunday, of course, and there would be church, of course. Behind Uncle Huw, there was the shadow of Edward. We had forgotten that he even existed. We tore through the covered yard, nearly knocking over the mangle, and into the hall where Stella presented us with her second trophy of the morning, Uncle Huw's underpants. 'Ach y fi, Stella,' we said. Outside the bells were starting – *come to ch-urch, come to ch-urch*. Stella is a mongrel and the retriever part of her tells her to fetch items of clothing from bedrooms. No one has taught her this – it is in her blood. But we were wolves wolfing down toast and bacon and milk and Auntie Maggie had the radio on singing hymns and the hymns were clashing with the bells and Edward was asking us questions like how many weeks we were staying but we couldn't even think. At last, Phyllis came down in a red, floor-length sun-dress and said, 'Just toast for me, please, Auntie Maggie. Hello, Edward.'

Edward blushed and got in a fluster and then pretended it was the beginning of a cough.

'Have a banana,' he said picking one out of the fruit bowl and pointing it at her like a gun. David and I looked at one another and cast our eyes up to heaven.

Then Uncle Huw said it was time to go and we gathered in the hall and Auntie Maggie whipped off her overall to reveal her best summer costume with mad, pink roses printed all over it. All she needed was her hat and handbag, which she fetched from the downstairs loo. Money for the collection? Right. Stella was shut in the porch in a state of great consternation. The bells were going even faster and we were running along and stopping and waiting for Uncle Huw and Auntie

Maggie to catch us up and Edward was asking all sorts of questions about time again that we didn't know the answers to. I was afraid we would be too late for the service and wasn't everyone there because the bells had stopped? Phyllis was drifting along as if she hoped we were too late but then we saw the vicar dashing through the churchyard, his cassock flapping and his bald head gleaming in the sun.

'Don't worry,' said Uncle Huw. 'No show without Punch.'

Another man in glasses exactly like mine but without the patch said, 'Welcome one and all,' in the church porch and gave us our hymnbooks and then came the organ and the smell of flower arrangements and sunlight on wood. We scrambled into our pew and there was a lot of kneeling on hassocks and bright stained glass and coughing and sneezing and then the vicar was in his pulpit and we were all singing, 'Now Thank we all our God'.

I thought we were happy. But some of us were and some of us weren't.

CHAPTER 6

When Eira arrived at the museum on Monday, Henry was sitting in the back room in near darkness. On a dull morning, like this one, it always felt as if night were about to fall in the museum, as if the order of day and night had been reversed. From the back, he looked like a lump of black rock. There were long fluorescent strip-lights hanging from chains which Eira turned on, one by one, so as not to blow a fuse, and, one by one, they hummed and boinged into life. She crossed the room and stood beside his chair, knowing what must have happened because it had happened before when Daisy had gone to hospital. Last time, Eira had heard him on the phone talking to her, saying that it was not to be, it was just not meant to be. 'Daisy, I cannot take away your pain,' he had said.

He had not opened his briefcase so far this morning. Eira put her hand on his green, cable-knit shoulder, her touch so light that he may not even have known it was there. Like snow falling gently on something dark. He smelt faintly of garlic, freshened by the outside air that had settled on him as he walked through the park. She thought of him, last night, dining alone while Daisy lay white and outstretched on a bed on her own in a room above him. Eira saw her hand tremble on the forest green wool. But she knew Daisy was not dead. Of course not. She would never die. Not Daisy Lux, in whose arms she had once seen Henry so fiercely gathered at the park gates, in this very cardigan she had knitted herself. Eira suspected that there were booties and hats and little blankets now to be stuffed to the backs of drawers. Either she would recover, as she had before, or she would not recover. If she did not recover, Henry and Daisy would be forced to part. In all the times she had met Daisy Lux, in various polite tea rooms and French cafés, they had never talked about children, never about babies. Sometimes, one or other of them would break off from what they were saying to stare at a baby in a papoose or a little girl singing to herself. But they never spoke of babies.

Eira went to make Henry a cup of coffee. It was not to be. It was a mistake. Miscarriages are Nature's way of getting rid of her mistakes. That is what people say. It would be a mistake for Daisy to have his child because their love was on the rocks, because she had turned him into a black rock by asking him to take away her pain. Eira put the coffee down on the desk. Once or twice, he had got their names mixed up but this time he didn't. He said, 'Thank you, Eira.' Now he had opened his briefcase and was making a pretence of sorting through some slides, fanning them out on the desk and peering at nothing through a hand-held viewer.

She went out to the main gallery of the museum and made sure everything was ready for visitors, in case they should have any, and started taking all the things out of the letter cabinet so that she could remove the fine layer of dust that had accumulated around them with the little brush that Henry had given her. All the time she was wondering if the baby's mother would come back, if the baby was in good hands, what would happen to the baby. In her fingers she held a sheet of yellowed paper that had been written on when the museum was still a house. She knew these letters well. She felt she knew the people who had written them. 'Dear Sir . . .' 'Dear Madam'. First they were acquaintances, then they were courting. 'Dear Ethel, might I call you that?' 'Dearest Josiah . . .' Then, eventually, as another winter grew into another spring, they were married and came to live under this roof with the whole of the park as their garden. Then there were no more letters because they never spent a night apart. Never a night alone. Like Mr and Mrs Lux. She went back to see Henry. She found him with his big, black head in his hands. When he realised she was there, he picked up a pen and drew a squiggle on a pad as if it were the answer to everything. The answer. If only she knew the answer.

At elevenses he said, 'Our cat has died.'

'Oh, no . . .' Eira said. Poor, darling Henry Lux. On top of everything else. 'If there's anything . . .'

At tea time, he came to find her.

'Yes. There is something.'

At the end of the day, they closed the museum together. Eira stood, her heart jumping, and waited while he put on his jacket and wound his familiar navy scarf around his neck. They had never left the museum together like this and she had never been invited to his house before. She had only met Daisy in public places, in polite tea rooms and French cafés. She and Henry only saw each other under the museum roof. They had never even walked in the park together because they approached the museum from different directions. She did not want to go to the Luxes' house at a time like this or ever. She did not want to see how they lived. As they walked along blossomy streets, just like those on her side of the park, she thought, of course I like walking with you and the way our footsteps rhyme, but I cannot speak to Daisy. Please don't expect me to do that. I don't know what to say. She will be crying because she has lost her fight to keep her baby inside her. I don't know what to do when other people cry. I don't want to cry. I cannot say the word 'baby' and I cannot take away your pain, Daisy Lux. But as they turned into a little overgrown garden with cascades of bruised magnolia petals and a sprouting privet hedge, and Eira was

41

looking up at the black painted front door expecting a sad, wan Daisy to open it, he said, 'Daisy has gone to her mother's in Staines.' And then he scrabbled his key in the lock as someone will scrabble, Eira thought, when they are drunk, perhaps, or because they are nervous, with a key in the lock, when they are about to ravish you in the hall. Ravish me. Please.

Jeoffrey was wrapped in a beige jumper on the sofa in his last, sooty slumber. There was a fish smell. Eira saw some curling smoked salmon in a little dish on the rug. Henry apologised about the fish – Jeoffrey's luxury, untouched last supper – and drew back the curtains. Of course, the room was exactly the sort of room Eira liked, with books and rugs and candlesticks and paintings of the countryside and the sort of furniture she would have chosen if she had been Mrs Lux. 'I am such a housewife!' Daisy always said, carelessly, even though she was an opera singer with an international reputation. And they do spend nights apart, thought Eira. Ha!

As for Jeoffrey's funeral, there was an understanding that Henry would do everything and that Eira would just be there. First, they went through the higgledy-piggledy kitchen, past red casserole dishes, heaped-up recipe books, onion strings, a draining board piled high, to the back door and opened it onto the garden. She waited on the steps while he fetched the body. The garden was a blizzard of petals, very right for a burial. She stood listening to the sweep of distant traffic and to the birds fussing in the privet hedge while he got out a spade from the garden shed, the dead Jeoffrey in the crook of his arm. Some children were playing, too small to be seen, behind the trellised fence. Henry started digging in a space in the centre of a flowerbed, among the roses. Eira hoped he wouldn't get into trouble. The earth was very dark and moist, like chocolate cake. Henry dug until he was out of breath. Eira thought, the sadness of his lost child has possessed him and he is pouring it all into Jeoffrey's funeral.

'Let me,' she said, and she went forward and took the spade and felt its unexpected, yet familiar, heaviness and dug hard until the spade hit something. It was a root. The hole was very deep now, almost too deep to dig from ground level. Darkness was beginning to fall. Eira looked up. The root must belong to the cherry tree. It was like a cradle made of two old, stiff arms. She stopped and jammed the spade into the ground and Henry took the cat and laid him gently down inside, not caring that his knees were going to get all wet and soily. A robin hopped about. Eira thought that Jeoffrey would have killed this robin without qualm and that the robin was probably singing because he was glad the cat was dead. Henry arranged the old beige jumper, drawing it gently over the gorgeous, dead, black face. Eira did not want to be the one who started piling on the earth. Henry drew from his pocket a small volume of poetry.

'It won't take long,' he said, although, in the end, it did take quite long. Eira stood a little distance away and sometimes Henry's voice petered out and there was the hush of cars and wind and the children playing, and sometimes she heard it very clearly coming to her . . . '*for he can creep . . .*'

At last he was able to say, 'He had a good innings. I will plant a Chinese lantern to mark the place. I have always wanted one.' And the idea of the bright orange lanterns and the black fur and the black soil made Eira think of tigers. They heaped back the earth and Henry put two sticks in the shape of a cross on the soil and a stone at each corner. 'Very soon,' he said, 'we will erect a more permanent and fitting monument.'

They washed their hands at the kitchen sink, sliding the bar of green soap between them. She wondered if he ever bought Lux soap. There weren't many people who were called Lux.

'Lux,' she said. Then she fainted.

She felt herself being carried somewhere in his arms and when she opened her eyes she was lying where Jeoffrey had lain on the sofa and Henry was looking into her face. *You are like a piece of light to me, Eira.*

'I'm sorry,' she said. 'I don't know why I did that.' Although inside her she did know. Deep down in the earth of her, she did. 'Perhaps it was because I was hungry.' And it sounded as if she had said angry.

Because the fridge was empty, he took her to the nearest place they could have a meal, which was a deserted Greek restaurant full of cheese plants and mournful singing. They didn't talk about Daisy or the miscarriage or Jeoffrey dying and she did not tell him about the baby she had found on the museum steps. All the time Jeoffrey was buried in the cold earth, and Daisy was in Staines and the beginnings of the baby Daisy had left behind her in the hospital were burning in the incinerator and falling as ash over Tottenham. And Jack was in the arms of a new lover half his age. And the museum was in the middle of the park, like some sleeping monster, while all the people were locked out of the park because it was night. Maybe the museum wasn't very good for either of them, but museum business was what they talked about since they didn't know how to talk about anything else. She said that she had never imagined that she would work in a museum, so shut away from the world (which was perhaps the longest thing that she had ever said to Henry Lux), and he asked her what she would really like to do, but she pretended she didn't know and stabbed herself with a fork under the table so she wouldn't cry because 'mother' was the only word she wanted to say. She felt almost beautiful in the candlelight, although of course she knew she was far from beautiful because she hadn't got her contact lenses in and her hair had bits of grey in it, and Henry looked distinguished and handsome because he was. On the way home his phone glowed with a message from Daisy. He read it, smiling sadly as he put his phone back in his pocket.

'Daisy is a rare person,' said Henry Lux. Eira watched their matching footsteps on the wet pavement and knew that he loved her, whatever he might say about Daisy.

'It is so sad,' Eira said, and Henry looked at her with his burning, tigerish eyes. At the corner of Sylvan Avenue they said goodnight quickly and went their separate ways.

The next day there was a headline in the local weekly newspaper: MYSTERY WOMAN ABANDONS BABY AT SURGERY, so she started wearing a different coat and changed her route to the museum and wondered what would happen.

CHAPTER 7

E dward Furnace took over our attic. It was perfect for him because he could shut himself away and concentrate on his book. His book was supposed to be a secret, and it was bad manners to mention it, but we all knew he was writing one. It is awful to wonder what has happened to that book. Auntie Maggie says in the olden days the attic was servants' quarters but that was long before her time. I expect it has always looked pretty much the same. Neither she nor Uncle Huw goes up to the attic ever because stairs are bad for knees. I had always liked the attic as it's plain and I used to feel calm there, although I wouldn't now. The walls are palest pale pistachio green and there are two metal single beds standing on the bare floorboards and no rugs and it's quite echoey. There's a rocking horse that doesn't rock any more because Uncle Huw rode it to death when he was a boy in another house, somewhere I have never been. The window-sills are deep enough for a game of Monopoly and long enough to lie on, twice the length of this window-seat in the junior library, where I'm sitting now. The window-sill in the attic is where I used to lie two summers ago, and the summer before that. I liked the feel of my back, smooth against the cool, painted wood. You can't see the garden if you are lying down but you can hear voices, if there is anyone there, quite clearly. You feel more associated with the sky. You listen to the buzzards mewing. You watch clouds travelling. You hear the rush of leaves near your ears and water down in the river and all the sheep crying and sometimes the cows when they go splashing and mooing into the water. Auntie Maggie and Uncle Huw never worry about where you are. I used to lie there for hours on end doing Sweet Fanny Adams. Before Edward came.

I knew it wasn't Edward's fault that he took over our attic. I had seen him give Auntie Maggie his rent, a roll of notes she put in the teapot on the mantelpiece in the kitchen, so it was quite fair. But I wished he didn't have to sleep there. One day, I crept up his stairs. I didn't want them to be *his* stairs. He had gone to play golf with Uncle Huw as though his book didn't matter a jot. Auntie Maggie was in the kitchen with David demonstrating how to pluck a chicken, which didn't seem a very good idea for someone with asthma. Phyllis was mysteriously out. I crept in bare feet. He had been sleeping in the bed near the wall. There was a faint cidery smell because Auntie Maggie used to store cooking apples under the beds before her knees got bad, and they might even have been still there rotting for all I knew. But stronger was the smell of him: his man's skin and man's sweat (I don't know why Auntie Maggie always called him a boy) and his sleeping breath and his smoky smell. I imagine he didn't open the window much because of the bluebottles that come in from the spinney. Auntie Maggie might have struggled up there just the once to prepare his room, more likely she had asked Phyllis to do it or perhaps Phyllis and Edward had done it together. I don't know. She had given Edward a cane bedside table with a white cloth with butterflies on it made of holes, and a bright orange lamp. Someone had hung up a picture of Mary and the baby Jesus and shrouded the rocking horse in an old curtain so it was just a grey lump. The biggest change was that there was a desk made out of an old door balanced on some tea chests, and in the middle of that was a green typewriter that said Hermes on it, heaps of books and papers and a round glass ashtray jam-packed with cigarette ends. It was hot and stuffy because the sun was beating down on the roof. I could feel the sweat prickling in my armpits. Phyl and I sometimes used to play Maids in the attic, and I was so nervous about trespassing that I heard Phyllis's voice saying 'You be Elsie and I'll be Violet' and I thought she was actually there and I actually turned round but, of course, she wasn't there. Anyway, we were too old for that.

Edward was a twenty-two-year-old man, despite what Auntie Maggie said about him being just a boy. His man's jeans and man's denim jacket were lying on a chair, his camera, his record player, his records, his books, his green bottle of aftershave. On the bedside table there was a book with a picture of a cobweb on it called *Dr No*. In the typewriter was a sheet of paper with some words I didn't understand and next to the typewriter was a photo of a girl. That's when my stomach flipped. David was calling me, thinking I must be in the garden, to go and pick gooseberries. I backed out and half fell down the stairs. I found David with Auntie Maggie in the fruit patch at the same time as a clap of thunder. Auntie Maggie gave me a metal bowl.

'Will I be struck by lightning?' For my sins. For trespassing.

Auntie Maggie said, 'Lord love us, no!'

The gooseberries thudded into the bowl and the thunder grumbled but the rain never came and it carried on getting hotter. As we ran inside for lunch, I saw Uncle Huw and Edward getting out of Edward's Hillman Imp. Edward saw me and waved and my stomach did another flip. After the flip there was something else. It was like the paint that plumes out into the water when you clean your paintbrush – all the colour swirling round until it breaks down into the water and becomes a part of it and the water just looks dirty. All inside my stomach. That's what it felt like.

At the lunch table Uncle Huw said, 'Who wants to come with me to see Mrs Pryce?'

Lettie Pryce is someone Uncle Huw used to visit after she lost her husband. She lived on the other side of Priestmeadow. Last summer, Auntie Maggie had told me that Uncle Huw and Lettie had what she called 'a fling' during the war, before she and Uncle Huw got married, but Uncle Huw didn't know she knew about it. 'Mum's the word,' I'd said.

'Actually, it's the gooseberry jam this afternoon, Uncle Huw,' said David because he had made a prior agreement to help Auntie Maggie. Auntie Maggie smiled, a little sadly, I thought. Phyllis didn't answer and glanced out at the swing. Edward looked down at his crumble. He usually went upstairs to his room in the afternoons, to write. Phyllis would just want to be lying on the swing reading. She was always reading, swinging back and forth and not hearing you when you called her name. But at least she hadn't officially stopped speaking to me then.

'Me and you it is,' Uncle Huw said to me.

'Keep an eye on him,' said Auntie Maggie, but only I knew the significance of that.

I love going anywhere with Uncle Huw. We were both ready to go as soon as Uncle Huw had found the golfing umbrella in case it rained. It was too hot for outer garments. He filled his pipe as I slipped on my sandals and off we went with Stella at our heels. The first part of the journey is down the main street, where Uncle Huw had to keep stopping to talk to all his old pupils. To get to

Lettie Pryce's house, you have to walk right through Priestmeadow and past the dairy and over the river and then down Long Lane and then through a field and her house is on the edge of the woods, not far from Maude's cottage.

Lettie Pryce had a long-haired dachshund called Tam. Tam could do all sorts of tricks, like lifting a paw and rolling on his back and saying 'woof' because Mr Pryce had taught him. Lettie Pryce opened the door and stood for a moment with her hands on her hips while Stella and Tam sniffed each other's bums.

'Well! What a surprise,' she said. But I don't think it was a surprise unless she meant I was the surprise. Lettie's face is like a crumpled up brown paper bag but her hair hasn't gone white, as Auntie Maggie's has. It's dark blonde and I don't think it is dyed, even though Auntie Maggie says of course it is. She wears it in a sausage around her head and she still puts bright red lipstick on like people used to do in World War Two. It always looks as if she has tried to draw on a new mouth, as if she thinks her real mouth is not big enough.

'Good afternoon, dear Lettie,' Uncle Huw said, and we followed her into her house, which is a large bungalow with a garden of fir trees and evergreen bushes and rockeries arranged all around it, and inside she had shelves of coloured glass flamingos and giraffes that sometimes caught your attention even from the garden when the sun shone from one side of the house to the other.

She never looked miserable about losing Mr Pryce. The tea things were always laid out nicely, as though she liked living by herself. It has always been summer when we visited her, because I am only ever in Priestmeadow in the summer, so she always had slices of lemon to go in the tea and not milk, like normal people have, and what she called orangeade for me in a green glass jug and a tin of Fox's biscuits, though there was never cake. This particular time, I spent the rest of the visit in the garden taking Tam through his paces on the obstacle course that Mr Pryce had set up for him before he died, and rewarding him with bits of ginger snap while Stella lay in the shade looking sad and bored. Everything I did in the garden I imagined they were watching. The garden was like a grass stage with fir tree curtains and I was performing for them and Tam was performing for them but I never looked in the direction of the window, despite what Auntie Maggie said about keeping an eye on Uncle Huw. I wanted them to think that I was not aware of them watching me at all. When it was time to go, Lettie tapped her rings on the window and Uncle Huw stood up behind her and I slipped back through the sliding door, with Tam and Stella on either side. This time, I thought, Lettie has been crying about losing Mr Pryce; I can see from her blotchy eyes and her real mouth is showing.

'She has quite a talent with dogs,' she said, and I wondered if I would end up working for a circus.

On the way back down Long Lane we saw a kingfisher swoop down the river. I had never seen a kingfisher until then – a flash of blue, like a tropical bird.

'I wonder if Mum and Dad have had any luck spotting the warbler?'

'Let us hope so,' said Uncle Huw, and then he said that, as a boy, he once saw seven kingfishers sitting on a branch – young ones learning to fly.

'I can't beat that, Uncle Huw,' I told him. 'I don't suppose anyone in the whole world can.'

When we got back to Priestmeadow, big, fat splats of rain started falling and we stopped in the churchyard to put up our umbrella. Stella ran onto the bank and frolicked among the gravestones so Uncle Huw told me to catch her and put her back on the lead and, when I had got her at last, we all stood there for a while huddled under the umbrella. I could hear Stella panting in time with the rain and smell the metally smell the rain made as it touched the warm tarmac path.

'Poor girl,' said Uncle Huw. I thought he meant me, or Stella, but then I saw he was looking through the rain at an old, leaning-over gravestone that I had never noticed before, all on its own near the yews. 'One day, I will tell you the story of Mary Evans,' he said.

'Who was she?' I wanted to ask. But I didn't. I decided to wait for him to tell me in the fullness of time. Which he didn't.

When we got home, there were thirty jars of

warm jam on the kitchen table and David was drawing in a scrubbed space in front of them. Auntie Maggie had gone out to the library and Edward was working, apparently. I noticed that Phyllis was wearing eye make-up. Mum and Dad were totally against make-up but Auntie Maggie and Uncle Huw have poor eyesight so they probably thought they were her real eyes.

'I'm just going upstairs,' Phyllis said, wrapped in a flowery bedspread from the garden swing.

David passed me a clean sheet of paper and said, 'I'm drawing a Welsh dragon.' So I drew a damsel in distress.

CHAPTER 8

Eira had always thought she would never go back to Priestmeadow. But on one of her days off, a few weeks after finding the baby on the museum steps, she did go back. It seemed the only thing to do. Even though it was only April, it was so sunny that the church door was warm beneath her palm. But inside the porch it was as cold and as dark and as damp as ever. She opened the inner door, drew back the curtain and stepped into a white-arched silence. There was the familiar, sharp smell of hymnbooks. From the high windows of the nave, wide planes of light fell through dust onto the terracotta floor. Above the altar, light burned through a dark blue sky, the white body of Christ, the scarlet clothes of Mary Magdalene. Eira lifted up the wooden font lid and peered into the bowl of pale stone and thought of all the babies that had been held above it – the cries of babies, the splash of water, the old stone darkening and then drying back to white. She walked the length of the nave and climbed the pulpit steps and looked out over the empty pews. Inside this church, the secrets of Priestmeadow still swirled about, trapped in long-lost prayers beneath the ancient beams of the roof. Outside, there was the permanent sun, the moon and the stars, and the earth as it is in heaven.

She went back out into the warmth, to the gravestone set apart from the others on ground that was unconsecrated two hundred years ago. There was a jar of browning daffodils that someone sentimental had left as though it were a recent grave. They seemed as pointless as flowers on gravestones always seem, however long the dead are dead. She crouched down to read the words that she had first seen twenty-six years before: *Here lies Mary Evans, who Suffered aged 17 years. He that is without sin among you let him first cast a stone at her.* Her fingers touched the rough indentations of the letters; she was feeling the cold now beneath the shaded secrecy of the yew tree, smelling the dark earth of winter that the spring sun could not reach. It was Maude, not Uncle Huw, who had told her the story of Mary Evans in the end.

She walked out of Priestmeadow to the old house. Uncle Huw had sold up years before, not long after that last summer; she had no idea who lived there now that he and Auntie Maggie were both dead and gone and buried in South Wales where Uncle Huw had been born. In her mind, they still occupied that house. If she could go in and sit down by the fire, they would be there in their cracked leather chairs, stoking up an argument of one kind or another. She wandered back through the town and out again the other side, a walk that passed the edge of the woods. She didn't want to go inside the woods. She kept walking along the road until all the warmth of the day had gone and the wind picked up in the trees and bowed their branches and made the crows caw and fly up into the air like fragments of soot. Then she turned round and skirted two tangle-edged fields until she ended up at the gate near Maude's cottage. It was where she and Maude had first met when she was a child. She had come then and sat on this same licheny gate and the curly-headed cows had stared at her from beneath their long, white eyelashes. In her pocket had been a postcard from her father about a sighting of the warbler they had nearly almost had. And Maude had appeared, as people do sometimes appear, when they are most needed. It had been here, in this little gateway, only it was summer instead of spring. The earth as it was in heaven. These fields all tucked around Priestmeadow like fuzzy green and gold blankets.

And Maude came again, now, and found her in the black shadow of the hedge and led her into her cottage with a strong hand. Maude, who had come to Priestmeadow as a girl from a bombed grey Coventry and for whom Priestmeadow was always a refuge and always would be. She had made her cottage and her cottage garden a haven. She had learned more about local history than the people born and bred here. She liked a good story.

She had kept hens and she had a beehive and she grew vegetables and fruit in her garden and she had worked in the library and she was kind. She had no husband and no children, but she was not lonely.

They stopped in the middle of the path in a band of sun and put their arms around one another clumsily. Maude must have been nearly eighty now, her face collapsing under the weight of years, but her eyes were still the same. Miss Sharp Eyes is what Auntie Maggie had called her. Eira wondered what Maude could see in her own face, what marks were left there from the years with Jack. The years without Phyllis. Eira told her about the museum in the middle of the park with the lake and the café and the knickerbocker glories. But she didn't say anything about the baby she had found on the museum steps, and she said nothing of her lonely passion for Henry Lux.

CHAPTER 9

I think about David all the time and I wish that he would write to me here at Maldwyn Girls. I know that a letter from David would be very short, and mostly in pictures or codes that might take a lot of working out, but I would like this because it would be something to do. I seem to finish my prep too soon. The things that I can do in fifteen minutes take the others an hour because they are always whispering and underlining their titles with coloured pens. But the teachers say: 'It's not a race, Eira Morgan.' David has had his eighth birthday now. I made him a card from leaf rubbings and the leaves were trees and I drew birds singing in the trees, but then I realised I couldn't post it because Phyllis is looking after Mum and Dad's address and she is not speaking to me, so I tore it up. I wonder what a Fijian birthday is like. The tree-house was his domain when he was at Priestmeadow in the summer. Do they have tree-houses in Fiji? Janet says no, they don't. Not particularly. When we were in Priestmeadow, I'd hear the floorboards of the tree-house squeaking as he looked out with his binoculars towards the town and the hills beyond, north, south, east and west, from the safety of the leaves. There is one hill which looks like an elephant lying down. There are no elephants in Fiji, Janet says. I liked knowing he was there. I knew he wasn't watching me. In the tree-house he was turning the pages of *The Hamlyn Book of 1,000 Things to Make and Do* with his small, rough hands. For a moment, I seem to hear the scrape of his pages but it's only Janet flicking through the *Encyclopaedia Britannica* in the other window-seat. Priestmeadow is what people are forever calling a sleepy market town and even where Auntie Maggie and Uncle Huw's house is, not so far away from its centre, perched above the river, it's as quiet as any empty hill-side. Once, I thought I heard the trees breathing but it was actually David struggling for air.

David has lived his whole life suspended between health and illness. When I sat below him on the grass in those first few days of the summer holiday, doing my cat's cradle, my back against the trunk of the oak tree, I worried about him because in the summer Priestmeadow is one big bowl of dust and fur and pollen and grass clippings and hay particles. His illness is very different from Phyllis's because its causes are known. I feared that he had a vision of himself as an old-fashioned boy – a maker of catapults and whistles from hazel stems and a whittler of things out of wood, like Daddy or Uncle Huw. But he is not an old-fashioned boy

61

at all. He has never made catapults and bows and arrows and whistles and he can't make things out of wood. He only looks at pictures of people doing these things. He cannot be this wild, laughing boy. He makes strange houses for stick insects, quietly, and he draws pictures of mythical beasts, such as the Cyclops, the unicorn and the slithy tove, and he likes cookery. I thought: he is stilled, caught in the trees like some strange, brown bird who has no ability to fly. But he is not a bird; he is a brown-haired boy, whose skin turns dark gold in the summer and in the winter he is very pale.

I watched David helping Auntie Maggie in the kitchen. I watched as he took a knife to the edge of the pastry lid that she had thrown like an eiderdown over an enamel plate of sliced apples and sugar. He took the knife and he pared off the pastry as she had shown him and he made a slit in the top and brushed it with milk.

On a rainy day, Auntie Maggie sat us down at the kitchen table and taught us to knit. She had a book left over from what she calls 'my youth' with patterns for twin-sets and all sorts of old-fashioned clothes in it. I liked reading the captions under the pictures. One of them said, *Who cares if it snows? This vest and panties set is so warm you can laugh your head off at a north-east wind!* and there was a picture of a woman with sausage-style hair like Lettie Pryce wearing a pair of big white knitted knickers and a knitted vest. In the time that I had been looking at the book and waiting for Auntie Maggie to come back and help me because my wool had got stuck, David had practically knitted half a scarf. The wool made him cough just being near it. His scarf so far was a beautiful bottle green and purple but my wool was the colour of sick and I couldn't bear it or knitting, especially in the summer.

David said, 'When I have finished this scarf, it will be a hundred miles long and it will have all the colours of the rainbow in it like Doctor Who's.'

'I dare say,' I said.

CHAPTER 10

At Maldwyn Girls there is no such thing as too thin. According to Phyllis, you can never be too witty or too thin. Janet and I are sitting in the icehouse, sheltering from the October winds because the junior library isn't open at morning break. I am trying to work out when it started, when Phyllis's life became one big diet and she kept shutting herself in her bedroom and refusing to come out. I think it might have been before her O-levels. Janet tells me her mother locks herself in her bedroom when she's been on the sauce and listens to sad records but that her mother hasn't got any O-levels. Phyllis never drinks alcohol in case it makes her fat, and despite all the time she spent counting calories in the year of her O-levels, she got ten As. I don't remember her liking music much at all until this summer when she used to listen to Edward's transistor radio every single day. But she was fading away ages before that. It was all happening for so long without anyone doing anything.

'She was fading away,' I say to Janet at lunch time when we are sitting on The Stump, leaning our backs together. 'That's why my mum rang up Auntie Maggie. She was in despair, Janet.' Janet doesn't say anything. Janet really hates it when children call people they are not even related to their aunts. It really annoys her. When Janet gets cold her skin goes like the sort of marble that has grey veins in it, the kind they sometimes use for gravestones. Her home is in Scotland but she hates her home even more than here. Home is the last place she wants to go to on earth because she doesn't like her own mother. But it was my mum who started the auntie thing. She was evacuated to Priestmeadow in the Second World War and her real parents were killed by a bomb and Uncle Huw and Auntie Maggie took her in. She was hardly going to call them Mummy and Daddy.

'Why does Phyllis look Indian?' Janet asks as we are sticking the Vs up at the passengers of the one fifteen.

'Because she is.'

'How come? You're not.'

'I told you. She's not my sister.' I want to tell her because it is a story I like. But I don't. I want to tell her that when she was twenty-one, my mum went on a thing called the hippie trail and, once, she slept with an Indian man under the stars on the roof of his palace which was in the middle of a lake. All night in his arms, wrapped in a beautiful carpet. She had fallen in love with this prince at first sight but in the morning she realised he hadn't fallen in love with her at all. She went on

65

with her travels and she tried not to think about him but it was no good because something had happened that night that would mean that she could never forget about him. So she travelled all the way back to the part of India he lived in, which was called Kashmir, and at last she found a fisherman who would row her out to the palace and the prince greeted her with a bow and a mischievous smile as if he might be thinking about falling in love with her after all. But when she told him she was expecting his child his smile disappeared under his moustache, like water going down the drain. He said he could not countenance the idea of marrying her. Mummy said that it didn't matter about the marrying. What about the baby? And then he said something unrepeatable under his breath and Mummy said of course she couldn't, she couldn't countenance the idea. He rowed her back across the lake himself, through the water lilies, without a word, and she came home and Phyllis was born in Priestmeadow in the big, saggy bed that Auntie Maggie still sleeps in now. And on the plane on the way home she met Daddy and by the time they got to England they had fallen in love at first sight.

I go back to saying how Phyllis was fading away and how Auntie Maggie and Uncle Huw waited until she had done her last O-level exam and then they came all the way to London and rescued her. How Uncle Huw kept calling her a damsel in distress. How it was meant to be just for a while at Priestmeadow but a few weeks later, after David and I had broken up for our summer holidays last year, the whole family went to Priestmeadow for a visit and we could see she was getting fatter. And she had made a grown-up friend and his name was Edward Furnace and he was their lodger, although I didn't meet him until this summer because he had gone walking in the Peak District that year.

'What's he like, then?' Janet says, all nudge-nudge-wink-wink. But I don't want to talk about Edward right now.

'Just a man.'

I shiver. Instead, I tell her of the day two summers ago when Phyllis got her O-level results and my mother had her brainwave of Phyllis coming to Maldwyn Girls' College so she could have a whole new start. It was too late for a scholarship but they gave her a scholarship anyway. That's how clever she is.

'Cleverness is overrated,' says Janet, who thinks she is so clever herself.

I am still talking to Janet but she can't hear me because my mouth is not actually saying the words. I am stuffing her face with all the facts she wants to know so much but no sound is coming out of me. We are just sitting, glumly picking at leaves and acorns, or watching other girls playing in the distance. Sometimes I think, did I say that? Have I been speaking aloud all along? Can she hear my thoughts? Am I telling her the very things that Phyllis meant I should not tell when she said I must not breathe another word?

Every morning Edward Furnace used to drive her from Priestmeadow to the station in his car so she could go to school because she was a day-girl at first. And in the evening he drove her home. That's how they got to know each other. Janet looks down at her legs. They are doing the marble thing.

Then she was Cleopatra in the school play because she looked the part. After that suddenly she decided she wanted to board. It was what she wanted. I think I know why she did that now.

'Who in their right minds would board if they had the choice?' Janet said once.

This summer, when that leaf you are tearing with your fingers was still green, Janet, my parents went on one of their bird expeditions to Fiji. Then they came back for a week. Just a week. They didn't know anything about what happened. And now they've gone back again and they've taken David because the climate is good for his chest. And I got a scholarship too and I don't know why because I'm not clever at all. I'm a stupid idiot. So now I've come here to be with Phyllis in her last year of school. And I miss her even though she is right here in the sixth form because she won't speak to me and she won't look at me and I miss Mum and Dad and David. I want to go home and I'm such an idiot because home is the only place I want to be on earth. Home is where Mum and Dad are so that means home is Fiji and that's much further away than Scotland. If I'd messed up the exam,

68

I'd be in Fiji now. But I didn't mess it up so I have to be here not talking to you.

'But why has Phyllis sent you to Coventry?'

'That, I cannot say.' I make it sound as though I can't say because I don't know why.

Janet has to go and have her violin lesson. I watch her weave through the grey mass of girls, the violin case bashing against her stiff little legs, and then I go to the junior library and stare out of the window at the grey sky and all I see is a summer's day.

I'm looking out of our bedroom window. It's the day after David and I arrived and she's lying in the middle of the lawn. Auntie Maggie is weeding in the corner of the garden, throwing dandelion clumps into the barrow. Stella is lying a little way off gnawing the marrow out of a bone. David is in his tree-house and Uncle Huw and Edward are inside. She's there in the centre of the lawn. The lawn is a bleached, bumpy green. The mat could be a raft on a pale green sea. She's lying on her side in this big, red, floaty, gypsy kind of dress she found in the dressing-up box. Not thin now. All that is over, we think. Fingers crossed. She's not exactly sun bathing, she's just lying all covered up in her layers of material and bedspread with her head pillowed on Edward's transistor radio. She's known Edward for more than a year. I am looking down on her from the bedroom window. I can't manage to open the window catch and I

69

don't want to knock on the window, because then David and Auntie Maggie will see me too, but she won't look up. An old Sunday magazine is still on the same page it has been this last hour, curling and flapping in the wind. I press my hands against the glass until I can't stand it any more and then I run down the stairs and crash into Uncle Huw in the hall. 'Whoopsy!' he says. I run across the prickly grass on my bare feet and lie down beside her and she opens her eyes and looks into mine. *It's a heartache, nothing but a heartache*. She turns up the song on the radio. She looks at me. There is a blankness – as if she has sailed so far away on her raft that she doesn't even recognise me.

'Eira,' she says, but deadpan. Like she means, 'It's Eira. No surprises there.' But there is a tiny, very tiny, thing that is so tiny it's not even a sound or a pause on the end of my name. It is only just there, a ghost of a question, as if she could be about to say, 'Eira? There's something I want to ask you.' I say her name back to her just the way she has said mine: 'Phyllis'. As if there is a question in my mind too. Something that I cannot say. We go through the magazine doing, 'What would you like on this page?' In this game you can have anything – a pair of jeans, a house, a kitten. I point to a knee with perfect skin on it. To a pair of green eyes that don't need glasses. She points to a girl running down a beach away from the camera.

'I'm knackered,' she says.

The song has changed to 'Bye Bye, Baby'. A boy

cycles up to the gate and whistles. We all look. Phyllis rises up, leaving me with the quiet song and the bashing of the soily weeds in the barrow and David rustling and creaking. She trails over to the gate, all in her red, and says something and he laughs and then she floats slowly into the house and he goes and sits on the grass bank. I watch him swigging Dandelion and Burdock from a big glass bottle, pulling at the long grass. Up in the bedroom, I can see shapes of clothes being hurled around, but she comes out wearing what she was wearing before, all frills and flounces and shawls. All raggle-taggle gypsy. She grabs her sandals and wanders off, still barefoot. Auntie Maggie has moved to weeding near the gate and she eyes the boy through the bars. She has known him since he was a baby. His name is Matthew Finn and he is as blond as Phyllis is dark.

'Back by tea!' I hear her say.

When Phyllis has gone, David comes down from the tree-house and follows Auntie Maggie inside as obedient as any good dog and Stella wrinkles her brow anxiously watching them, because she is not a good dog. I want to know where Phyllis is going and I think how she is better since she has started going to Maldwyn Girls' College. And yet not better. I think Edward must have wanted to know too because here he is, his dark shadow falling across the magazine. He smiles at me and I see his face upside down so it looks like a potato with a mouth and his spots are the eyes of the potato. He is carrying his camera and he wants to show me how it works but I don't want to know how it works so I don't listen. His breathing is very close and he smells of smoke and man's hair. He tells me he is going off to take some landscape shots and I dread him asking if I want to come too but he doesn't.

'Landscapes,' he says again, then he hangs the camera over his shoulder like a lady's handbag, lights one of his disgusting cigarettes and saunters off.

CHAPTER 11

Eira was on her way back to London after her visit to Priestmeadow. She looked away from the crammed train compartment and watched the blue hills disappear as the train rushed on, leaving the Welsh borders far behind as it plunged its way through the bright green landscape of England. Until now, Priestmeadow had been untouchable, dark. A bright place fallen into shadow. Now, the shadow was lifting.

Until she had written to her, Eira had thought she would never see Maude or Priestmeadow again. She had imagined Maude was dead and buried like Auntie Maggie and Uncle Huw. She looked out of the window at a vast, pale sky and thought that she did not ever want to be buried herself. She wanted her own ashes scattered somewhere, somewhere she didn't even know yet. She saw a man who could have been Jack and who could have been Henry Lux walking with a little box of her ashes, up a winding lane and through an orchard of white apple blossom.

The first time that she had met Maude, when she was a child, in the gateway of the field opposite her

73

cottage, with the curly cows looking on, she had been scared of her. They had gone down the path through her garden that led to her cottage, and the flowers on either side of the path had been so tall – monks' hoods, hollyhocks, big daisies that seemed as tall as trees. Sitting on the train now, looking out at Carpet World and United Biscuits and the ranks of lined-up cars and factories, she saw her ten-year-old self from the outside, how Maude must have seen her. She looked across at a girl at the opposite table, drawing a picture. She had only been a child. Only a little girl. A reflection of the lined skin beneath her eye flashed briefly in the dust-smeared window of the train.

Just a girl, standing outside a cottage one afternoon in early July over twenty-five years ago. A day of brightness and shadows. An aeroplane, an old-fashioned one, with a sputtering engine, had strayed from an air show. She remembered its sound and it merged with the sound of the train. She could have been her mother standing there, on another July day during the Second World War. A child far from home, enclosed in a fold of green summer countryside, safe from bombs, but all her world lost and nothing ever the same again.

CHAPTER 12

I lie awake at night in our dormitory. The shapes of other girls' bodies surround me like graves. I don't feel safe in the dark but in the dark I can remember things more clearly. I am thinking of a day in July. It's bright and the wind keeps changing the clouds. Brightness and shadows. A low-flying plane. A pattering of sound. The leaves are rustling in the trees, the warmed yew giving off its special scent. I follow a woman through a garden of sweet peas, roses, red-hot pokers. I don't know she is Maude yet. I am afraid of her. There is the smell of lavender and hot rosemary and bees are sailing in and out of a white-painted hive all by itself on the grass. The cottage door stands open and inside it is black. There is a strange smell coming out of the kitchen.

I think that I will run away but I can't. I feel drowsy. The woman has disappeared, leaving me in a little room with everything miniature – a flowery sofa and curtains; tiny books the size of pockets with dark blue covers and gold writing on their spines; a wooden box with two carved birds on it; pincushions, and a picture on the wall of a milkmaid in a field that looks as if it was painted a long time ago but could be the field outside the window where there are some sheep grazing now. It's so quiet you can hear their teeth tearing up the grass. There is a jug of sweet peas on the window-sill. A small clock is ticking. The woman comes back with a tumbler of something yellowy but she doesn't say what it is. She carries a plate piled with dark brown slabs of cake. I am not hungry. I am thirsty but I dare not drink the yellow liquid in case it is poison. I find myself sitting on the chintzy sofa and the material is cool against the sore backs of my knees. A floppy cat comes in and jumps onto my lap.

'That's Tabitha Twitchett.' The cat is soft and easy to stroke. I am afraid to eat the cake.

'I was just making a pot of tea,' says the woman, tilting her head to tell me to follow her into the kitchen. Further, deeper. 'I'm dyeing.' I stop stroking the cat. There is no air to breathe. I slide off my cushion and follow the woman into a back kitchen that is too hot and too dark with green, seaweedy strings hanging from the beams. On the Rayburn there is a cauldron steaming and all over the table there are nettles. I think I will be stung to death or made to knit a coat of nettles like the girl whose brothers were turned to swans. I wait.

The woman says, 'I am dyeing sheep's wool and I'm going to spin it myself. What do you think of that?' She has done some with gorse already. I know you can dye eggshells with gorse petals for Easter because I've read about it in Enid Blyton books. I know too that when gorse is out of bloom, kissing's out of fashion and that means kissing is never out of fashion as you can always find gorse in flower. Auntie Maggie told me that. The woman leads me into another room with a polished dining table and a fireplace and there is a real spinning wheel like the thirteenth fairy's. I am thinking of a castle and a tall hedge made of nettles and an Indian prince who is stung half to death because he does not love his own daughter. The woman has a brown Betty teapot and some teacups with pink roses on them that look like dolls' cups.

'Aren't they dear?' she says because she sees that I like them. The woman has an old-fashioned way of speaking and a dress that looks as though it has been dyed as an experiment. She is wearing dusty Wellingtons even though it is such a sunny day.

'Are you a tea drinker?' the woman asks, her hair a big flock of grey question marks around her head where wisps have escaped from her bun in the heat, in the steam. I shake my head. I've got a headache and I think I should tell her that I ought to go home because what if Uncle Huw gets there before me?

'I'm only staying with my auntie and uncle,' I say, to show that I am not important.

The woman puts down her cup. 'I'm Maude. I hope you'll come again. It's called "cut-and-come-again cake" – won't you have one little piece?'

'My name is Eira Morgan. I am only here for six weeks, for the summer.'

'That is quite a long time.' And then, after a pause, she says, 'I work in the library.'

Auntie Maggie goes to the library. 'Do you know my auntie?' I pause, feeling myself sweating. How to explain her? 'She's got white plaits that she winds round and pins on top of her head?'

The woman smiles as people always do when they think of Auntie Maggie. 'Yes! Yes. I do. Maggie. I could ring her up now and tell her you are on your way home?' We look at the dusty black telephone on the window-sill. I wonder about Uncle Huw and whether I have let him down by stopping here. I have not done as I was told.

'No,' I say firmly. 'I must go.'

The chapel clock is pinging three on the other side of the quad. A blast of wind comes down from the Maldwyn hills and rattles the drainpipe outside. It's strange I had never noticed Maude's cottage before, set back from the road. As we walked back down the path through the garden, a sudden wind swept over us and then Uncle Huw appeared walking past and I could hear him singing.

'*You are my honey . . . honeysuckle, I am the bee . . . I'd like to . . .*'

'Hello.'

'Hello, my dear,' he said kindly. Maude leaned on the gate and smiled, still holding her delicate pink-flowered cup. 'Ah. You've stopped off to see Maude. Afternoon, Maude.'

Uncle Huw held out his hand for me to put mine in and I did. He seemed tired after comforting Lettie such a lot. I squeezed his hand and he squeezed mine back. Maude had already turned and was walking back up her path, her hand flung up behind her in a vague goodbye, throwing her tea leaves on the garden.

When we got back, everything was quite calm and ordinary. David had done an amazing picture of the most beautiful exotic bird you could ever imagine and he had called it a Krake.

Uncle Huw said, 'Long time since I have heard a corncrake.'

I could see Auntie Maggie's feet in ankle-socks and sandals from the kitchen window and David explained she was cleaning the outside windows because she needed to let off a bit of steam. Edward was trying to talk to Phyllis on the swing. I went and found them. Edward's face looked hot and red, nearly as red as the big red sun-dress itself. Beyond the gate I saw Matthew Finn, whistling, cycling round and round and round in a cloud of dust.

CHAPTER 13

The Luxes had invited Eira to a party. 'Only a small gathering,' they said, to mark Daisy's thirtieth. So now she was walking through the park, just before it was locked, wearing her contact lenses and her best green Chinese dress and with her red lipstick on, carrying a bottle of un-chilled wine because the fridge in the off-licence was broken. She averted her eyes from all the babies. Baby after baby after baby. Her pace had to be brisk to overtake the laughing couples swaying about in each other's arms and blocking her way. It was not because she was hurrying towards Henry Lux. It was not because her heart was beating faster the nearer she got. She ignored the museum, all shut up and dark, as though she had nothing to do with it. No one loitered there after-hours, looking like the lost mother of a lost baby. No one had come when it was open. There was no new box on the step, no person where the box had been. She had wondered again and again what had happened to the baby and where the baby was now. Her own abandonment of the baby had been a crime and a sin.

She arrived at the house with its big, black door and knocked, hearing faint music. He opened it at once, which was not what she had expected, and stepped back, beckoning her in. Daisy swooped forward plumply and took her hands and kissed her cheek. She'd never kissed her cheek. He didn't kiss her cheek. Daisy smelled of a passionate perfume and was very much in demand. Henry wandered away to get Eira a drink. In the party there were more couples. In the room where Jeoffrey died they were bunched up on the sofa, cradling their drinks, murmuring over the music. She could smell the food in the air and the wine on their breath. One couple looked up exactly together as she entered the room as though their necks were on the same elegant hinge. And down. Henry came in behind her and handed her a glass of icy wine. He seemed about to introduce her to someone but then he got distracted and forgot. There was nowhere to sit and the glass doors were open onto the garden with steps leading down. They'd set out some garden furniture but it was all deserted, glasses left here and there. She walked straight out, as though to admire some flowers in a long trough, and then she saw the end of the sunset and pretended to be admiring that. She was gathering her thoughts, drinking, gathering her strength, drinking, trembling at being there in the garden of the Luxes, wishing the Luxes had never met. A man with straight brown hair and big shadows under his eyes came out of the undergrowth, smiling at her or to himself, it was not quite clear. She looked away at the delicate bells of a clematis, deepening from mauve to purple in the beginning of the dusk. For a minute, she'd thought that it was Jack.

'I like their cat's gravestone,' said the man. 'At least, I hope it's a bloody cat.'

'Why?' she said, feeling possessive over Jeoffrey's grave and that she should have seen it first. Henry should have told her it was there.

'See for yourself. Before it gets dark,' he said, looking back at the rose bed and smiling again, this time definitely at her.

'Thanks. I will.' Eira was hoping the man would go away, off into the house to talk to someone else, and he did, which was nice of him, and when he had gone she went inside the house as well, so as not to seem too eager to follow his instruction to look at the grave.

After an hour of hovering around the edges of other people's conversations and bumping into Daisy still passing round canapés as light as air that she said she had made herself in her higgledy-piggledy, housewifely kitchen that morning, Eira walked as far as the grave. She lit a match, read that it said, *For he is the Tribe of the Tiger*, and thought that, yes, it was a good gravestone. When she returned, the man was there again on the steps, lighting a cigarette off the last one he had been smoking, which Eira thought excessive of him until she realised she had stolen his matches.

They were all coming out of the house now because they wanted to smoke more because they were getting drunk. But she was in the garden for a more cowardly reason: inside there was Henry Lux. And Daisy, back to her big old self in her big pink velvet dress and her big silver bangles and her big breasts and her big-teeth smile. Making everyone feel at home with her canapés and her passionate perfume. Now she was curling on the floor at Henry's feet so he had to stroke her hair, so shiny and hennaed, so utterly devoid of grey. Her skin was smooth and coffee coloured. She flexed her neat, strong ankles in time to the music, as though warming up for the performance of a dance. Apparently, later, she was going to sing; her friend, Julian, who was probably famous, would accompany her at the piano. Now she was showing everyone the kitten Henry had bought her for her birthday, a jumping-jack of grey fluff she had named Silver. To have waited such a short time after Jeoffrey's death seemed unseemly. To get a kitten when everyone knew you wanted a baby was pathetic. The apples were forming on a branch of a tree that overhung the fence, tiny fists of compressed flesh, and below them there were tulips going softly black.

'I said, now!' Daisy laughed, stamping her pretty foot at Henry, who was juggling drinks. She was going to sing now. Now! There was a flock towards the piano. Julian in position. All was hushed. Julian began. She began. When she sang, her voice became not her voice any more. It was beautiful, of course. The beautiful song of Daisy Lux, lamenting her lost child, Eira decided, since she couldn't understand Italian. She knew that really she was singing about love but that was worse to think about. How could she sing about love when her baby was dead? Why didn't people sing as children do with clear voices that sound the same as their speaking ones? It was all affectation. And did any one of those people craning in around her at the piano understand a word?

The aria ended and, while everyone was clapping, the chain-smoking man with the blue eyes came to where she was standing, still in the garden, and said, 'What's up?'

'Men always say that.'

'Sorry.' He took a slug of his drink and crunched up the ice.

'Sorry,' she said. Through the windows, she watched Henry go out of the sitting room and appear in the kitchen. She thought, perhaps if I go in now, if our fingers touch as he gives me another glass of wine, or if my body brushes his, or if we look at each other straight in the eyes, for once, or he notices my green Chinese dress, my red painted lips, and he notices me . . . The man followed her gaze, stubbed out his cigarette and walked away and back into the room to listen to the singing. Now Daisy was singing the blues. Eira went towards the others and leaned against the door frame. '*Come to me, my melancholy baby,*' sang

Daisy Lux. Eira's throat was tightening and she turned her face away until it was over, staring into the dark and the lights coming on everywhere in the houses all around. Someone in another house was doing the hoovering. A man closed a curtain as if he were about to make love. She went in and tried to talk to a woman who was in despair because she hadn't had a boyfriend for seven years. The woman was very pretty. 'Where are all the men?' said the woman. If she didn't meet someone to have a child with in the next year, she said, she would jump onto a train track. She had dismissed the man with the tired eyes and the crooked smile who had talked to Eira in the garden and whose name, it turned out, was Ray. Eira hoped he couldn't hear what the pretty woman was saying about him, about his teeth and how perhaps he could have them professionally whitened. The woman tried to draw Eira into a conspiracy against the couples who were now moaning about their children when they could have been dancing. Eira told the woman that she was sure she'd find someone when she was least expecting it because this was what people always said to her. The pretty woman looked as though Eira had slapped her.

Henry was getting a beer for the man waiting at his elbow who was telling him a boring joke and screening him from view. She helped herself from a bottle on the table and took the pretty woman a drink. Now the pretty woman was telling her story about wanting to have a child to another woman. The other woman laughed her head off. 'You've got plenty of time. Look at Cherie Blair!' Eira wandered outside. Even though she had given up smoking eight years before, she took a cigarette from a packet someone had left on the table and lit it because the alcohol was telling her to do stupid things. It tasted synthetic, packed with a thousand toxic chemicals, and it burnt a hole in the back of her throat. She felt someone beside her and turned, expecting Ray back yet again, but when she looked it was Henry. It was as if her desire for him had conjured him there.

'Hello,' he said. He was drunk.

'Hi.'

'Do you like Jeoffrey's headstone?'

'Yes. Very fitting.'

'Thanks for helping me that day. Did I ever say thank you? Don't know what's the matter with me lately.'

'It's understandable.' They drank their drinks. She wanted to seize him in her arms and kiss him.

'I don't know about that,' he said.

She basked in the thrill of being near him in this new situation, not in the museum, mellowed by alcohol. His body was so close. He was wearing a white shirt that he never wore in the museum. He smelt drunk and cinnamony.

'Henry?'

'Yes, Eira.'

'This really strange thing happened. The morning

you were at the hospital. It was so strange that I think I did the wrong thing.'

He looked at her. They sat down on the wall and she steadied him and she told him about the baby, about taking her home. She had never spoken to him like this. Because she had said the word 'baby' she was crying. She could feel the tears falling down her cheeks in straight tracks.

He stopped her. 'Eira, are we talking about the abandoned baby that was in the local paper? In the news? That was outside the museum? I had no idea! Fuck!' His voice was low. Babies were a difficult subject in this house.

'Please don't swear when speaking of the baby,' she said. 'I don't think anyone noticed what I looked like. But I should go to the police, shouldn't I, because then it might help them find the mother? Would it help them find the mother?'

'Eira, didn't you know? The mother came forward. It's okay.' He was stroking her arm now, trying to soothe her. 'Eira, it's okay. It's not even this week's paper. I read it some time ago.' She let him go on stroking her arm and she pressed her forehead into his shoulder, covered in the special shirt he never wore in the museum, and smelled him. She looked up, right into his eyes. It was too dark to judge the expression. She felt as if her body had been broken in half and the two halves were falling away from each other, maybe never to be reunited. He said: 'I'll go and get the paper. It was in the *Advertiser*.' He left her sitting on the wall. It was cold now. All she could think of now was going home to bed and going to sleep and forgetting about everything. Out of the corner of her eye she saw Ray swaying in the shadows. He came over and picked up her hand. She let it lie limply in the cradle of his palm. With his other hand, he was holding out a torn piece of a cigarette box with a telephone number written on it in large, sloping digits.

'I know you won't ever call me,' he said. Then he stumbled away into the room where the music had got deeper and throbbier and a few people were slowly dancing. Henry came weaving back with the paper. She took it and went to get her coat and Ray shut the front door quietly behind him.

'Thanks. I'll read it later. Thanks. I'm going home now. Thank you. Tell Daisy Happy Birthday, again.' She'd forgotten to even say it once. He said she'd gone to bed. Eira realised she hadn't even brought a card. For the first time she saw the other cards dotted around the room, the things that were gifts from Daisy's real friends. She folded the newspaper in half and put it in her bag. He helped her get into her coat, wrapping his arms around her in a sort of hug. The hall was empty, except for them. He took her face in his hands and looked at her and then he took his hands away. She breathed in his breath, sighed, slightly leaned towards him. He leaned towards her. That was all.

Ray's number was still scrunched in her hand

all the way home, all the way round the edge of the locked park. It probably wasn't safe for her to be wandering around by herself at that time of night, but she didn't care. All she had was another man's number, a man she had no wish to see ever again. She didn't have Henry and Henry was married. But Henry had wanted to kiss her. She knew that Henry had wanted to kiss her as much as she had wanted to kiss him. She thought of the Luxes in bed together, of Henry closing his eyes and imagining that Daisy was Eira and Daisy knowing nothing.

CHAPTER 14

I'm awake in the dark dorm but in my mind it is always the summer in Priestmeadow, bright and clear and hot. I'm in Maude's garden, sitting cross-legged on a cushion, level with Maude's dusty brown shoes and a stream of ants carrying our cake crumbs towards a crack in the path. 'Who was Mary Evans?' I say. Tabitha Twitchett stares at me and pricks up her ears. 'What is her story?' I ask because of what Uncle Huw said. Maude smoothes out an imaginary wrinkle from her dress. The broom pods are snapping open at the end of the garden, one by one.

'She was a servant girl from the Cadwalladers' old estate, out at Combe. Hanged in Priestmeadow in 1805. There's no house there now. It was all burned down. There's no nothing.'

'Why did they hang her, Maude?'

Maude stirs her tea and closes her eyes as she takes a sip and I think that she won't tell me. But she will. She will tell me part of the story every time I visit. In the first part, it is Christmas Eve in 1803. Outside, it is snowing. Inside, the Cadwalladers are eating their dinner. There is the father, the

91

mother and their son, William, who is twenty-two like Edward Furnace, and all his younger brothers and sisters and several guests who are friends of the family. Down below, Mary Evans is in the scullery. The kitchen is hot and full of Christmassy cooking smells and smoke and the clatter of pots and pans.

Each day, Mary gets up in the dark and goes to bed in the dark and hardly has time even to look up at the white, winter sky, except when she goes out to feed the chickens, or else to kill them, which she hates. It's too cold to stay out long and the ground is slippery with muck and snow and ice. She has never seen the rooms upstairs where the silver and the patterned china are laid out, where the chandeliers that the other servants talk about are, and the tiger skin, as big as the duck pond. She thinks she would like to touch the tiger skin. More than that, she wants to touch William's face because he is so handsome. But she is only the under-cook and her hands are rough and raw. It is the stable boy, who smells of hay and horses, who says he wants to marry her. 'Come up to the hayloft,' he says, 'and I will show you something you've never seen before.' Never a day goes by without him asking. Never a day ends without him making his rude remarks and teasing her until she cries.

Each morning, Mary dresses in the dark with numb fingers. Works in the scullery. Goes out into the spoiled snowy yard. The house is dark. William

Cadwallader is somewhere inside it. She wants him for herself. She wants the stable boy to leave her alone because he stinks.

'She wanted too much,' says Maude, putting down her knitting.

Every day, before dawn breaks, Mary stares at herself in the blackness of the scullery window and imagines things. On her very first morning, before she had even reached the house, she had seen William in the yard, walking his horse to the stables. She had curtsied and when she had looked up he was smiling at her. He had raised his hat and looked into her eyes. She had looked into his. As she walked on, she looked over her shoulder and he was still watching her. That was when the wanting started.

'That's all it took,' Maude says.

Then she had stepped out of the light of the yard and into the kitchens. The chopping and scraping had stopped. She had seen the cook put down her knife. The cook had seen what had happened through the window. Mary had felt dizzy and curtsied and bowed her head and thought of her mother, just as she'd left her that morning, waving from their own cottage doorway with the youngest of the babies in her arms.

That's all Maude will tell of the story for one day. I run from her cottage, back through the fields, all through Priestmeadow, past Mary's grave, thinking about wanting, about wanting too much.

I stand in the long grass at the gate of the house, spying on Matthew Finn and Phyllis, at the way they are pressing their bodies tight together and their faces together. I rush past them and slam the gate behind me as hard as I can.

CHAPTER 15

Auntie Maggie washes her hair over the basin in her bedroom and combs out the tangles at her dressing table with a metal comb. Then she calls me. First, I help her to dry it with the hairdryer by holding sections of hair out in front of the warm air or by holding the dryer myself, especially round the back where she finds it difficult to reach. Sometimes, when it's warm, she sits on the swing and lets it dry in the sun and I just keep her company. She sits there in her petticoat slip, all wobbly-armed, and laughs about the other old ladies who have their hair cut short and have shampoos and sets at the hairdresser's and sit under those domes. She calls them 'the short and curlies'. Her secret is that she adds her own rosemary from the garden to the shampoo, so another of my jobs is to gather the rosemary from the herb garden and crush it in the pestle and mortar. If any bits are left in after washing, I pick them out. Then she parts it in the middle herself. Only she knows how to do it dead centre because only she knows the shape of her head.

When it is all dry, she lets me do the plaits. I love this because my hair is not long enough to put in plaits and it's the wrong sort of hair because it is too bushy, but her hair is just the right kind, smooth and thick and all the same length down to her waist, all white with not one strand of grey, even though once it was black as a Spanish lady's. Then she winds it round twice and pins it on the top of her head with a big tortoiseshell comb. Auntie Maggie says she would love to get her hands on Phyllis's hair. It looks almost blue sometimes, Phyllis's hair. If she wanted, Phyllis could have all sorts of styles but she only likes to wear it loose. I think it is like a big curtain that she hides behind. Even at Maldwyn Girls' College, even now, some teachers have given up telling her to tie it back because every time they aren't looking she lets it down again. It is like a Cape of Disguise.

One day, Auntie Maggie asked me to take her books back to the library. She found me a basket to put the books in and I decided I was going to take Stella out on the lead to stretch her legs, so I'd got Stella in one hand and my wicker basket with the books in the other. Stella was pulling because she hates being on the lead, but I have to put her on it if there are no grown-ups, and I was struggling along when Edward came up behind me and offered to take my basket to the end of the lane. He said he was going out for some inspiration for his book. If Edward mentioned his writing himself, it was not bad manners to talk about it so I told him that I really hoped he found some. He'd got his camera again so he could record anything important and I could see his notebook poking up out of his pocket.

Everyone seemed to be going out that day. Phyllis and Matthew had disappeared at lunch time, murmuring about a boat. Neither Uncle Huw nor Auntie Maggie was concentrating. I thought, if Phyllis drowns, then they'll be to blame. If Mum and Dad had been there, they'd have been insisting on life jackets and arm-bands – but then it was their fault if they decided to leave their children in the care of a couple of seventy-five-year-olds for a whole summer. Uncle Huw was out now but I didn't know where, although I had my suspicions, and Auntie Maggie and David had gone to buy cooking ingredients.

By that time, I knew that there was definitely something wrong with Phyllis. She seemed all right when she was with people but when she thought that no one was looking, the light went off inside her and when I asked her a perfectly normal question like 'What did you do today?' or 'Can I come with you?' sometimes she couldn't even answer. At the end of the lane, Edward returned my basket so he could branch off on his own and I continued on with the books and Stella. 'Can you manage, pet?' he said. There was something so nice about him sometimes and yet that feeling in my stomach would keep coming back again whenever he was near.

The library is my favourite place in Priest-meadow, especially on a hot day. It's cool and quiet because most people think that if a hot day comes you have to go outside and get burnt. Except David and Auntie Maggie. That day, they were making the Christmas cake. Auntie Maggie said the earlier the tastier and she would jab it with a skewer and feed it with brandy from then until Christmas day. She must still be feeding it now. After that, Auntie Maggie was going to let David see the photograph collection. The idea was to find as many interesting things to do inside as possible because if he went outside too much he'd probably have an asthma attack. I thought there were plenty of things inside that could set David off, such as boxes of dusty photos, but David was looking forward to it so I didn't say anything.

It made sense for me to go to the library since I'd made friends with Maude. I had instructions from Auntie Maggie to collect some books on herbal remedies and plant folklore that Maude had ordered for her, and Maude went into the back to look for them. There weren't any other borrowers there but Maude was different from how she was in her cottage and so I was too. It was a question of distance. I went to the children's section where there is a small green table and chairs set out. I'd got my own library tickets and I could get three books, so I found the next two Penelope Livelys that I hadn't read and then I looked up Fiji in the big red atlas. Fiji is very small and it's next to Australia. Last time, Maude had said that the only thing she knew about Fiji was that they had mangrove swamps and that the capital was called Suva. Now, she had found something else.

'Look,' she said. It was a book of Fijian bird paintings. I opened it and started to turn the pages carefully. Each bird was marvellous in its own strange and distinct way. They had their names underneath: Reef Heron, Grey Goshawk, Pacific Golden Plover, Velvet Dove, Peale's Pigeon, Collared Lory, Yellow-breasted Musk Parrot, White-Rumped Swiftlet, White-Collared Kingfisher, Pacific Swallow, Polynesian Triller, Island Thrush, Spotted Fantail, Black-faced Shrikebill, Vanikero Broadbill, Blue-crested Broadbill, Scarlet Robin, Golden Whistler. They were paintings but they were real at the same time. I wanted to show it to everyone. Maude said that I could take it home for a week, but only a week, because it was really a reference book. A little bit of the writing caught my eye. It said the man who painted the birds was called Mr William Belcher. It said that he enjoyed taking his own children for nature walks along the beach and through the bush. It said: *The miracle of colour in a dewdrop on a leaf would excite his interest and break the long silences his family remember.* I stored these words in my heart. Some other people had come into the library so I let Maude talk to them and then I went up to the desk and she stamped my books. She'd already done Auntie Maggie's and put them in the basket. Maude lets Stella go outside to a little courtyard at the back of the library where she keeps a bowl of water for her, so I went and collected her.

When I got back, I had the garden to myself. Uncle Huw isn't a big fan of hot weather either; I could see him in the snug, his newspaper held over his head like a big kite. Phyllis was still out. I knew Edward would still be out too as his inspiration walks took a long time. I thought that Phyllis and Matthew could be down at the weir, where everyone swims in the cow-mucky water. I knew Phyllis wouldn't have gone swimming herself, though. She never goes swimming because she says she's too fat, although no one ever disagrees or makes a fuss when she says that. I think we should say, 'No. You are not fat.' But none of us ever does. A boat would be different, I thought, because you could keep your body covered up. Perhaps Matthew's family had brought a boat down the river from the farm.

I climbed up to the tree-house because I liked getting a chance to go there by myself. I took up the bird book and one of the herb ones, but I was saving the Penelope Livelys so I left them at the foot of the tree. I wanted to look at the bird book before I showed it to anyone else. I made the birds fly off the page so they were all sitting round me in the tree singing. Auntie Maggie wanted the herb books to try to find a cure for David's asthma, so I looked up asthma and it said you could make an infusion out of hyssop or marjoram. The other one was a folklore book that people used to use to cast spells. Auntie Maggie was probably thinking that she could apply some magic to the situation. I flicked through the pages, looking at the black and white illustrations. It was full of tricks that young girls used to do to make men marry them.

There was a splash from the river. I looked out with the binoculars that David keeps on a hook. Phyllis was drifting by like Cleopatra in her barge. I was surprised to see that she was being rowed not by Matthew, as I thought, but by Edward. My heart sank. Trust Phyllis to end up being his inspiration. My stomach started doing its mad flipping thing, like a fish turning over in a net. I went back down to find Stella lying under the tree on my books, chewing them. Uncle Huw was coming out just as I was coming in. He whistled and Stella went skidaddling after him. I left my books to dry. Uncle Huw was only going for a wander and a smoke in the garden but he likes Stella's company more than anyone else's when he is doing that so I left them. Auntie Maggie was so pleased with her books that she got out her glasses and her magnifying glass and set about looking through them straight away. David was watching television with the curtains closed. He smelt of Vicks VapoRub. I put the bird book on his lap. He didn't say anything. He looked miserable as he opened it but I knew that he would like it very much and that he would use it for ideas for his drawings of made-up birds.

When I went back into the kitchen, Auntie Maggie said she was going to kill two birds with one stone. I left her to it, knowing I had to sneak up to Edward's attic again. After seeing him in the boat with Phyllis I had to. I felt sick and trembly as I went up the stairs. It seemed the same, only this time there was writing in the typewriter that I did understand, all crossed out with Xs. Underneath the Xs it said, *From between your legs your wetness coats my fingers like honey*. There was the photo on the desk of Phyllis, like before. I wanted to cover her up. There was the musky, man's smell in the room.

I went back outside, for a walk, but I didn't know where I was going exactly. I walked through the spinney. It was so gold and warm and the light was full of tiny insects churning about in the air and all the dust and pollen that is so bad for David. There was no boat going by any more and I wondered if I had dreamed it. I put my hand down my pants and felt between my legs but it wasn't wet. I wandered along the edge of the river and then I trailed back through the town. Maude would still be in the library. I wanted to hear the rest of the story of Mary Evans. Perhaps if I went down Long Lane I would find that Uncle Huw was coming back from Lettie's and I could meet him halfway.

CHAPTER 16

'Thanks for coming,' Henry said, when she hadn't said anything about the party after a couple of hours. Maybe, if I had just kissed you, thought Eira, we would know where we were. If that kiss had been kissed. Neither of them mentioned the baby conversation. She had read the article. The mother was fifteen, living with her grandmother. They were finding it difficult to cope. The girl had thought it was a baby clinic because her grandmother had said it was – all the old people still called it that. The girl and her grandmother used to wheel the baby past the ducks in the park. The girl thought a baby clinic would be a sensible place to leave the baby and so she had crept into the park secretly before school. The baby was called Fatima but Eira couldn't remember what the girl or the grandmother were called. She could only remember that the grandmother was forty-six. They were back together now, all smiles. End of story.

'Good,' said Eira. 'Everybody's happy.' Then she chucked the newspaper in the bin and left for the museum.

That day, Henry had done a lot of talking. He'd told her in great detail about the exhibition panel they were going to do on the history of the park's gardens. He'd talked for ages to an old man in a Homburg hat, who wandered in from the park, about the old days in Southgate and how things weren't what they used to be and he had agreed that it was a crying shame. He had showed some children the beehive, where there seemed to be some new activity, and told them about the complete life cycle of the honeybee, how honey is made, from pollen to the moment it is ready to spread on our toast. He said a lot of other things but it was all just museum business. Then he stopped being talkative and a glum silence fell between them.

'Did you enjoy yourself?' he said at last, as though he hadn't spoken to her at all at the party itself, as if the moment in the hall had not happened, as if he had forgotten about the abandoned baby completely. As if he were only now getting a chance to ask her. He said he was so drunk he could hardly remember what had happened later on, even though Eira knew he was no more drunk than he might be expected to be and nowhere near the blanking out stage.

'Yes, thank you. I had a lovely time. I hope Daisy enjoyed herself,' she said.

She felt his eyes upon her as she passed the window on her way out for her lunch-time walk and when she looked up, yes, there he was staring at her. He gave a careless wave. When she got back, there was a woman dressed in black sitting on the bench in the vestibule. She was holding the baby in a paisley shawl with a long fringe. She smiled with shiny, wet eyes and Eira nodded and smiled back. Then she took a deep breath and peered over the top of the shawl. The woman jiggled the baby roughly as though she wanted to wake her up.

'No,' said Eira. 'Don't wake her.' The woman didn't speak much English. She kept smiling and jiggling. Then the girl ran up, wearing her school uniform, her hair scraped back so hard it made her eyes curl up at the corners. She took the baby straight off the woman and kissed her extravagantly, talking in what might have been Kurdish. Then she came up to Eira and said, 'I made one hell of mistake.' The grandmother scrabbled in the bottom of a shopping bag and brought out something wrapped.

'Something for you,' she said. Eira became aware that they were still in the entrance hall, but she wanted to stay where it was light. Henry appeared, looking on, pretending to be re-stocking the leaflet rack. She unwrapped the gift. It was a picture of the baby in a frame. The frame was chunky gold and inside was the picture from the newspaper of the girl with Fatima in her arms, beaming, and the grandmother. Two round, black pairs of eyes in the photo. The baby woke up and now there were three pairs, seeing if she liked her present.

When she looked at it closely, she could see that the picture must have been taken in the park itself. There were the lake and the ducks in the foreground and, very faintly, the grey shape of the museum could be made out against a slightly darker grey sky. She glanced up. They were all looking at her smiling, three smiles. Henry was not smiling. Perhaps he was thinking of his own lost baby that would never be found.

'Thank you,' she said. The girl had to get back to school so she gave the baby another big kiss and ran away.

They came back every so often after that. The grandmother more than the girl. Sometimes Eira would be at the front desk, or busy with her back turned, or listening to Henry, and she would become aware of them. Just there. The grandmother would bring the baby up and sometimes the baby would be awake, looking silently, or sometimes she would be grouchy. She changed moods every visit. Then Eira would see them sitting in the café having a knickerbocker glory or walking round the lake. Sometimes, the girl would appear from the direction of the children's playground and she would always kiss the baby as she had done on that first day – more passionately than you would do if you hadn't once thought you'd lost your baby for ever and it was your own fault. After a while, they stopped coming at all. Perhaps they had moved to another part of London. Eira wondered why they hadn't come to say goodbye but she knew that it is not always possible to say goodbye.

A month had passed since the party. Her feelings for Henry were reaching new heights. Once, she caught herself panting when he squeezed past her in the Long Gallery. The weather was getting warmer and the museum felt like a prison of coldness and dark. Daisy started coming to the park to meet Henry at the end of the day and they would go home the long way and walk through the rose garden. Eira hid in the office and watched them in the distance. Sometimes she went to the cinema with friends she had known from university still living in London, or went round to their houses. She didn't know anyone who wasn't in a couple or anyone who had no children. Even the gay ones had children. At first she had known one or two women who didn't want any but, after a while, even they had babies as well. One of them told her it was just to see if she could. Eira thought: for some reason train tracks do not appeal to me. For me, it would be to fall from the top of a high building, down into the earth, down to hell. As she went about her work at the museum, Uncle Huw seemed constantly to pluck at her sleeve, his growly, teachery voice quoting *Paradise Lost*, the fall of Satan . . . *from morn to noon . . . from noon to dewy eve. A summer's day.*

At night, in the dark, she saw a girl at a window high in the wall of a London hospital. The girl looked down from the window at the city and abandoned her childhood. Only then did she see that there were other figures, alone in other windows, framed by their own fear, confronting the glittering lights of the city and their own darkness. Far below on the street, people came and went. They seemed oblivious to the hospital. Unaware that from high above the city a girl was falling. Melting and burning, through her own deliberate fault, and falling unnoticed into despair.

In the queue at the supermarket she saw that there was a message on her phone. She listened as she packed her shopping with one hand, but she didn't recognise the voice. She played it again. It was Ray. One of the Luxes must have given him her number. She felt compassion for Ray Archer. He probably didn't really want to go out with her. He wouldn't if he knew what she was actually like, if he could see her close-up. She could picture him smoking in some darkened flat, thinking how he would just give it one more try, how he had nothing to lose. The sad woman with the green dress and the bright red lips. When she got home she played the message again and her finger hovered over the delete button. The man with the shadowy blue eyes. 'I'm sorry, Ray,' she said as she switched off her phone, 'but my heart is full of Henry Lux and there is no more room in it.' She saw herself and Henry standing beside an eight-tiered wedding cake and all the beautiful people she had seen at the party, except fat Daisy, and except Ray, who was not beautiful anyway, looking up at them from their tables. She was laughing through her tears and saying to them, 'Of course. Of course I loved him. We loved each other all along. What did you all think?' And they all understood.

CHAPTER 17

I am back there again in Priestmeadow. Here at school in the library, yet there at the same time, in my thoughts. There, it is raining. A heavy summer rain that may never stop falling. We sit around the kitchen table and the rain creates a feeling of safety inside the room, a safe cocoon. When I look for that feeling at Maldwyn Girls' College I cannot find it. When it rains here, the classrooms are dark as caves and the water drips and leaks through ceilings and they turn off the power because it is dangerous. And I am afraid of the dark, now. But it wasn't safe in Priestmeadow either. It was a false sense of safety that the rain created. It is never safe anywhere.

We sit around the kitchen table. David has taken over my bird book. He is combining wings, beaks, crests and talons to create a new bird of his own imagining. He has got the book propped up against the radio and is drawing in front of it, his felt-tipped pens strewn around him. I am also drawing. I am drawing herbs from life. I went out before the rain to fetch the rosemary for Auntie

111

Maggie's hair and I could see the rain coming in from the hills in a bank of grey. What Auntie Maggie so gaily calls the herb garden is not like the herb gardens they show on the covers of the herb books, with neat segments divided by box hedges and brick paths; it is just the bit of garden around the swing, spreading out from the bottom of the vegetable patch, and there are wild flowers that grow there as well. Auntie Maggie says there's no difference between a weed and a herb, between a wild flower and a weed. I go mainly on smell. If it smells interesting, I pick a small stem with leaves on it and put it inside my pinafore pocket.

'Good Lord love us!' Auntie Maggie laughs. 'But there will be a use for them all,' she says, 'and most of them can go into the chicken stuffing.' When I have drawn the herbs and looked them up in the books, I will write down their names in both English and Latin to practise my handwriting. In the past, people have compared my handwriting to insects' legs. I sharpen my pencil. Stella and Midnight are sleeping peacefully, Midnight on the boiler on a square of old carpet, and Stella under the table. I rest my sock on the dome of her head and when she growls in her dreams I can feel the vibrations through my sole. Uncle Huw is in the snug watching the cricket and we can hear the commentary, a low burbling and little ripples of applause, like birds taking off with beating wings. It is not raining at Lords. Edward is in his attic – or on the moon, for all we hear of him. Auntie

Maggie is reading the herb book with her magnifying glass and making notes about cures for asthma and eczema in her VG jotter, and today, wonder of wonders, Phyllis is actually here with us. She is sitting, wearing an old fishing jumper of Uncle Huw's, and so she's in the room, but not with us at the table. She's cross-legged inside the jumper, inside a big, brown, filthy armchair that is mainly used by Stella as a bed at night, and on her lap is a drawer removed, complete with contents, from a chest in the sitting room. She's got all the old photos that David was about to look at another day before they made him have a coughing fit. That's probably why she hasn't brought them to the table. Phyllis loves the old photos because there are lots of her when she was a baby. She keeps holding up pictures of herself as a baby, saying, 'Just look at me there!' and Auntie Maggie keeps saying, 'You were a wonderful baby. My golly gosh. Good as gold.' I shade carefully, damping my finger with spit and rubbing shadows. I don't know what kind of baby I was. Mixed in with these photos are all sorts of pictures of Auntie Maggie and Uncle Huw and Mum. Sometimes Phyllis likes to be a baby again. Auntie Maggie goes and sits in the armchair and Phyllis sits on the arm and they look through them together in a big cuddle. The rain shows no sign of stopping.

'Now, that's when I married Huw. Isn't he dashing?' Auntie Maggie says. 'Look at your mother. Such a brave soldier.'

There are no photos of David or me in this particular collection, except of our christenings and neither of us looks anything special – like white pupae, with all the ladies in flowery hats around us.

When I've finished my drawings, I reach for the book and start looking up my herbs. The book is called *The Magic of Flowers and Herbs* and it has a photograph of each plant and it says how to grow them and what they are used for. At the end of each entry there is a section about the magic side of things. I flick through the book. It says that some wives put caraway seeds in their husbands' pockets to preserve them from the clutches of other women. Honesty, like Auntie Maggie has in her flower arrangement on the landing, can be used for shape-shifting, flying, unlocking secrets and bringing the dead back to life. It says you can call butterflies by waving a sprig of lobelia in the air. I copy out the names and the Latin names underneath. I am not sure what to do with the pictures when I've finished. I hold them up for everyone to see, hoping my handwriting is not like the legs of insects.

'Ten out of ten,' says Auntie Maggie. I take them to show Uncle Huw and he says, 'You're a funny old thing, Eira Morgan.' When I come back into the kitchen I see that something has happened. Phyllis looks at me warningly as I come through the door.

'What?' I whisper. David looks up, as though for

the first time. Then he sees my face and looks back at Auntie Maggie and Phyllis and then back to his picture, tactfully. I approach the armchair. Now Phyllis is cradling Auntie Maggie who is holding a picture. One tear falls off the end of her nose and then another one off her chin. I see outside that the rain is stopping, as if the sadness of all the rain has turned into the drops that are falling onto Auntie Maggie's apron. Auntie Maggie always carries a proper cotton handkerchief somewhere about her person, with a violet embroidered in the corner, or an M, but today all her hankies have deserted her so I run to get her some toilet paper. I have never seen a grown-up cry. I don't like the way her face has changed, as though a horrible imp is stretching out her mouth with invisible fingers and she can't stop them doing it. When I get back, she's found her hanky and she's wiping her eyes and cleaning her specs. She doesn't say sorry or explain and Phyllis is still giving me her big-eyed, shut-up look over the top of Auntie Maggie's tortoiseshell comb. Auntie Maggie gets up and makes the tea in her little jig of clangs and whooshes and clicks, then she turns the radio on to her jaunty music and wipes her hands on her apron, as though she hasn't been crying at all.

'Take this in to Uncle Huw, there's a love,' she says to me.

When I go in, Uncle Huw has fallen asleep, so I put his cup and saucer on his little table next to his pipe cleaners and then I stroke the crinkly skin on the back of his hand and he slowly opens his eyes. The first thing he does is smile. I stand there for a while and someone catches the ball.

'Out for a duck,' says Uncle Huw.

'Auntie Maggie's been crying.' I feel like a tell-tale. As I say the words, I can hear that my own voice is very sad and shocked. I expect Uncle Huw to stagger to his feet and follow me back into the kitchen. I can imagine him picking her up in his arms and calling her 'old girl' and her laughing and shrieking, 'NO, NO, put me down!'

But he says, 'Oh, look, here's Midnight.' Hearing her name, Midnight gives a little squeak-purr and comes and jumps onto his lap. I don't like Midnight all that much (although of course I miss her now) because her fur is all manky and her breath smells, but Uncle Huw doesn't mind. His attention has floated back to the television and something exciting happens again and there's a cheer so I go back to the others and he doesn't follow me. Phyllis says Auntie Maggie has gone to have a lie-down.

It is getting brighter outside. We all keep doing what we were doing before: Phyllis making an album of herself as a baby, David still doing his bird. Phyllis has changed the radio station and a woman is singing about how she closes her eyes and counts to ten. The volume is on low. Phyllis is singing the words under her breath and licking the sticky corners that fix the photos in place.

I keep turning the pages of *The Magic of Flowers and Herbs.* Then I ask Phyllis why Auntie Maggie was crying.

'Come here,' she says. I go there.

She shows me a photo, which must have been the one Auntie Maggie was holding. Phyllis says she doesn't understand. It's a picture of a play and it's a funny, boyish Uncle Huw and a girlish lady in his arms. The lady is very pretty – tall and slim with long, blonde hair tumbling down her back with a sausage round the front and a dark mouth in what I know is called a Cupid's bow shape. And eyebrows like caterpillars. Uncle Huw has a massive beret and a tunic and a sword. There is a balcony in the background that has been painted on as scenery. I can see that Phyllis is upset too.

'Who is this?' Phyllis flicks the sausage hair of Lettie.

'How should I know?' I say. 'Romeo and Juliet?'

She puts the photo back and then she seems to get tired of the album and the photos and she goes upstairs as well. Phyllis was the actress among us, but I only know how good she is now that the summer is over.

I wonder if she is going to see Edward, if he's going to take photos of her, if he's going to put his hand down her pants. David's picture is fantastic. He goes to show it to Uncle Huw and then he stays and watches the cricket. Alone in the kitchen, I leaf through one of the herb books and arrange it lying open at a page of my own choosing in Auntie Maggie's place, where she was sitting, where she will read what is written. Finally, I get back to Mr William Belcher's birds. It's my turn and I take the book to bed. I play a game that I can take each bird out of the picture and that they let me hold them in my hands. I think about how William took his children on nature walks and how the miracle of colour in a dewdrop on a leaf would break the long silences his family remember.

In the night, I lie awake thinking about love again. It is beyond my experience. Why does no one love Maude? Why does everyone love Phyllis when all she does is moon around in a big jumper? Why does Uncle Huw love Lettie Pryce? I didn't know old people argued and shouted and slammed the door or that they argued about love. I hear them go into their different rooms and then there is quiet. I strain to hear if Auntie Maggie is still crying. I know that Phyllis is awake too.

'Phyl? Will everything be all right?'

'Course. Storm in a teacup.' We are quiet. Our tawny owls are calling to each other through the trees.

'I hate it when people argue,' says David unexpectedly. 'Birds don't argue.'

'Yes, they do. They dive bomb each other, like buzzards and crows.'

'Now we're arguing,' he says and coughs so much that Phyllis has to get out of bed and prop him up and rub more Vicks into him. I wish that

Mum and Dad would come home. In the morning, Uncle Huw doesn't say anything at the breakfast table. He eats his egg and then he storms out of the house without taking Stella. Stella sits in the porch and watches him with a furrowed brow until he disappears round the bend in the lane and then she sighs heavily and goes back to her basket. Auntie Maggie does so much cleaning that she has to send me out for more Gumption.

When I get back, Edward says, 'What did I miss?' But it is as if he knows, as if Phyllis has told him. He was not very good at acting. Not in Phyllis's league.

CHAPTER 18

There are three stages to Uncle Huw's return to us after what Phyllis calls 'the barney' and Edward calls 'the lovers' tiff'. The first stage is him coming home drunk. We are sitting at the dinner table, eating shepherd's pie, and the door bashes open and he is standing there doing his heart attack laugh. He navigates the dining room as if it is a galleon tossed upon cloudy seas, blind to us, but his eyes on Auntie Maggie as if she is his guiding star.

He sings, '*Come to me, my melancholy baby . . .*' and he laughs his laugh and cries his cry and lunges as if to kiss her but misses. She shies away from his breath, her knife and fork clattering from her hands. We are transfixed. Edward hops up and catches him. Draping Uncle Huw's tweedy arm around his neck, Edward leads him away, falling and stumbling and, after knocking over the honesty arrangement on the window-sill, he is taken off to bed. We wait. His bedroom door shuts quietly and Edward comes down with a red face, rather out of breath. None of us has eaten a mouthful since. Some of us have kept our forks in mid-air, where they were when Uncle Huw first appeared.

'He's gone out like a light,' Edward says, his green eyes resting on each of us as if to reassure us, but longer on Phyllis, when he should have looked at Auntie Maggie the most. I know this means that Uncle Huw's gone to sleep, and not died, but I don't like the feeling that the light has gone out of Uncle Huw. And even when people say 'gone to sleep' sometimes they do mean dead. That's what Dad said when our pet parrot died. Auntie Maggie hasn't said anything. Now, she just says, 'Forgive him.' Afterwards we watch *The World About Us* on TV and later Edward pops out. It is only just dark, the sky a royal blue as we see it from inside. Our holiday is running out.

'No doubt he's gone to find out what sort of trouble that silly man's been in this time,' Auntie Maggie says, jabbing her needle into her pincushion. But she's glad he came home in one piece. Last time, he fell asleep on the bench in the middle of the town and woke up with a fright when the milkman said good morning. It was too early for any of his old pupils to have seen him and that was a mercy, Auntie Maggie says.

The next stage is breakfast. When Uncle Huw comes down, he is all shaved and clean and pink and shiny-faced and his clothes are neater than usual, as though he is wearing his first ever school uniform. His hair, such as he has got, is neatly parted where he no doubt parted it when he was David's age. He eats his breakfast politely, carefully, and very quietly, so as not to draw attention to himself. Stella comes and rests her head on his lap and waits for crusts. Auntie Maggie comes in and out with pots of tea and toast in the toast rack and spreads butter and marmalade on her own toast and eats her own toast and sips her tea. Then, when the grandfather clock has struck nine, as though it is a signal, she goes up to him and gives him one forgiving kiss on the top of his head and everything is all right. When she does this, it makes me remember that Auntie Maggie has never had any children of her own and I wonder if she minds. Uncle Huw now springs into life. He's so happy to be forgiven he announces that he has a plan. He says that we're in for another burst of hot weather.

So, the last stage of his return is wild activity, a plan of some sort. The plan that he announces is a moth watch. Within half an hour, he is bathed in a sheen of sweat.

'What's a moth watch?'

It involves going into the garden at night and laying down a big white sheet and setting up a special lamp called a hurricane-lamp which will make the moths come out of the darkness, and then you make a list of what they are and you might see some unusual ones.

'We don't kill the moths, do we?' says David.

'Good Lord love us, no.'

'Doth the moon shine the night we watch our moths?'

'Don't be silly, Phyllis. As it happens, it is a full moon. Anyway, we have our lamp. If it is a fine night tonight, we will do it.'

He rummages around in the garage and finds the lamp and he takes it onto the kitchen table and makes it work. Auntie Maggie will find an old sheet in the airing cupboard and we will be all set. He goes out to buy the newspaper, bright pink with excitement, lighting his pipe, nearly setting fire to his trousers.

Edward has not interfered with their argument. He keeps a low profile and tells me that it is all good material.

'What do you mean?' I ask him, but he shuts himself away in his attic. Phyllis has gone out with Matthew. From the top of the tree-house I can see her in the long boat again, this time with Matthew at the helm, a cigarette in his mouth. Matthew's hair is so blond that it makes him a strange ghost against the dark summer leaves and shadows of the river. A god of the woods, I think. Later, I come across Edward reading on the garden swing while I am collecting herbs for a spell I'm going to cast to try to keep Uncle Huw out of Lettie's clutches. I am not sure whether I believe in the spell. I think that I don't believe it, but if it came true I would.

'Sorry to disturb you,' I say, tripping over Edward's size eleven feet, as I try to pick some parsley.

'Hello, pet. Can't you cool my fevered brow with your snowy hand?' I don't touch him, of course. I would be afraid to touch his skin because I am afraid of him. His face is cooking in the sun like a slice of bacon. I would be afraid of him feeling my rough skin too, my lizardy hands. 'What are you picking those now for? Don't witches gather their ingredients at midnight or dawn when the dew is fresh upon them? Or something?' I look at him. Trust him to guess I was doing a spell.

'I don't know to what you're referring,' I say, like a lady in a film I once saw.

'Look at the buddleia!' he says, suddenly. 'It's a purple hurricane-lamp!'

'Maude says it's a butterfly bush. Anyway, it is moths we are watching tonight.'

'What is the difference?'

'I don't know. They come out at night?'

'Have a look at their antennae, old lady.'

'I'm not an old lady and I'm not a witch, thank you very much.' I want to like Edward. I like the way his voice goes up and down like James Bolam's in *The Likely Lads*. But how can I, knowing what I know? I don't want to touch him. 'Get a hat,' I tell him and I go to find a quiet corner of the garden to say my spell.

I don't know what time it is when we go out, just that it's dark but also strangely light because there is a full moon, and then we are all there sitting on the edge of the sheet and the lamp is lit in the middle so that, when the moths begin to land, they land on us too. The garden is scenty and cool and magic. There is a faint wind. The light shines on our faces, making us have big hollows round our eyes, and everything about us is so full of shadows that I start to frighten myself by thinking we have all turned into huge insects too around this lamp and that maybe my spell has gone wrong and it will make something terrible happen. Or, what if, when Uncle Huw knocked over the honesty in the jug on the window-sill, he unlocked something that was secret? The sheet is soft and white underneath us. I am resting against Uncle Huw and David is resting against Auntie Maggie. They are on garden chairs and we are sitting in between their knees, using their lower legs as back rests. The owls are around us, very close in the garden, hunting ferociously because when the moon is full they can see their prey more easily. I think, suddenly, of the mice scurrying in the grass and how they will have nowhere to hide because their eyes are bright as jewels, when the moon shines on them, and they can't do anything about it. There is no need for us to be silent – it's not as if moths are going to be put off by talking. The light is so powerful they are drawn to it against their will. But we are silent. Hushed. I'm silently repeating my spell, because even though Auntie Maggie has forgiven Uncle Huw, it's not as simple as that. There's more to love than forgiveness, I think. There's Lettie and we've got to do something about the hold she has on Uncle Huw. She is a pretty owl and Uncle Huw is in her clutches. I wonder what an alien would think if it saw us. If a UFO landed and they all looked out with their big eyes and saw us here doing this. I often think about what an alien would think because the things that people do often look so funny from the outside.

These are the people who are on the sheet: David and Auntie Maggie on one side, then, going round clockwise, me and Uncle Huw with the moth book, and then Phyllis and Matthew, and Edward is taking up one whole side on his own. He's not on a chair but he's sitting on an upturned bucket, which I have told him is very enterprising of him. We're all being nice to each other, like that, as though it's Christmas or someone's birthday. We all want this moth watch to be something good. At first, I am worried that it's going to be a waste of time, but then they come, hurtling themselves at the lamp. Dropping and thudding onto the ground, onto the sheet, with whirring wings and spinning round like clockwork toys. Dazed, dazzled, in their furry, ghostly colours.

'*Bewitched, bothered and bewildered,*' says Edward.

'Don't touch them!' says Uncle Huw. 'Don't hurt their wings!'

So, the art is to look while they're there, which is sometimes not very long, but never try to hold them, never try to hold them in your hands, whatever you do. You don't want to kill them. But some of them kill themselves by diving into the flame and they burn to death and Phyllis tries to save them all the time, burning her fingers, and calling to them and telling them not to fly into the fire. We are all exclaiming and shouting and holding the book up to the light and saying, 'I think this is a Tiger Moth!' or, 'Look, look there's a Ghost Moth on your head!' and, 'I saw a Willow Beauty!' Although, Edward's just watching, like I am sometimes just watching. He's smoking a cigarette, which is not a good idea, because moths might not like smoke, and he winks at me. I don't wink back. I see Phyllis's and Matthew's heads bending together as they follow a moth crawling over the hem of the sheet, a beautiful one as big as one of Phyllis's eyes. And then one lands on Edward's nose, perhaps it was attracted by his Zippo, and it's a Death's Head.

It's probably not even that late at night, but it just feels it because we are outside doing this. I can smell the alcohol on the grown-ups' breath. Once, I see Matthew pick a moth off Phyllis's breast and she kisses his neck just leaning into the dark, only softly, a brush of wings, but I see. Edward goes inside.

Just when I am thinking that I never want the moth watch to end, the lamp goes out and Uncle Huw says he can't mend it when it does that and the show is over, folks. And it's suddenly very dark and cold. The moon's gone behind a cloud. I wasn't frightened of the dark then but I didn't like it. Not after the hurricane-lamp went out. We all go in, seeing our way by snatches of moonlight. Phyllis stays outside to shake the sheet and to make sure any of the remaining moths fly out into the night and to kiss Matthew properly. When we get inside, Edward is sitting at the table not doing anything, just sitting. Then we all gather round, grabbing the book from each other, round and round the table, and Phyllis comes in and half sits on Edward's lap and he groans. Uncle Huw ticks the ones we've seen in the index. He and Auntie Maggie are in love again now. I think of their love as being like the opening and closing of moth wings, so different from one moment to the next, so changing, the different colours of their love.

David and I went to bed. But later I woke up because Phyllis had come in. I watched her undress and I went back to sleep. It should have been a revelation, what I saw then. It should have been. But I didn't realise.

CHAPTER 19

The next Sunday, Eira found herself sitting with her family on an old bedspread in the middle of Hampstead Heath, wishing she had remembered her sunglasses. Her parents had positioned themselves at the two top corners of the bedspread, like weights, although there was only a little wind that day; David and his girl-friend, Jyoti, lay in the middle with their shoes off, tapping each other's feet in time to some secret inner song. Eira was at the edge – half on the grass. She drifted in and out of the surface of the conversation for a while and then she slipped underneath it altogether. The calls of children playing between some silver birches a few yards away seemed somehow more important, like notes of a tune in her own head she was trying to remember before it was too late. She watched her parents, squinting suspiciously against the sun, the steady rise and fall of her father's chest, her mother throwing crumbs to one of London's last remaining sparrows, a newspaper fluttering on her lap. David was talking animatedly about Jyoti, who was hiding her face in her hands and peeping through her fingers. Now that his asthma was a thing of the past, David was using all the energy he had stored up as a boy. He loved Jyoti because she was, he said, on the same planet. The planet of now, today, Eira thought, whereas my planet is maybe, if, if only, yesterday, maybe one day, should have, oh dear, now I am too late. As they had walked through the Heath from the car, David had told her he had asked Jyoti to marry him and she had said yes. Eira had put her arm through his and hugged him close to her.

'I am very, very happy for you,' she'd said, and she was.

David deserved happiness in a way that she did not. He would just think she was stupid if she said she was in love with Henry Lux and that she knew that some day they too would be together, that she had a feeling. It wasn't the same as saying you were going to marry someone for definite. So she told him about a coincidence that had happened the week before, when she had seen Ray at Paddington Station. She had watched at a distance as a girl came up to him and threw her arms around his neck and had been struck with a sense of loss. After the girl had gone, Ray had seen Eira too and waved and smiled but she had pretended that she was late for her train and hurried away. Now, she thought – despite The Great Dream of Henry – it was another chance she had missed.

David was only glad she seemed at last to have got over Jack. He gave her a hug and said she must move on and not blow it next time. Always move on. And, although he meant on from Jack, on from the possibility of Ray, his words made her think of Henry because she knew she was being stupid, really. Daisy Lux was a rare person, as he always said. I am not rare, she thought. I am cold and stupid. Stupid and cold and old and sitting on the edge of my life.

Phyllis was at the picnic too. Eira saw her in the clouds behind the trees, in the tottering yellow grass heads, in the curling bark of a silver birch tree. Worst of all, she heard her in the magpies calling from the tops of the oak trees, cracking out a message to the world that Eira was a stupid idiot.

Her father and David were talking now about colours, the qualities of each, the skill of turning them to your own ends. Her mother had brought something she was sewing or making, Eira could not quite see, but whatever it was, Jyoti seemed to know a lot about it, or she allowed herself to discover, to be drawn in, in a way that Eira could not. Eira was not a daughter any more, not the right daughter, not a wife, not a girlfriend, not a mother.

But she had been back to Priestmeadow now, and she knew she would go again. She watched children passing on the path nearby, carrying kites, laboriously pedalling tricycles, crying, talking, laughing, running, dancing. She brushed the crumbs off her lap and stood up. Over the brow of the hill were all the districts of London, seething and glinting in the sun. She heard her father call her name and glanced behind her. David and Jyoti were holding hands. They wanted to make an announcement.

On the Tube on the way home, she remembered another picnic. The only one they ever had during the last Priestmeadow summer. That picnic was a kind of peak of happiness from which there could only be a fall downwards: a falling off of happiness. Eira supposed they must have driven to the edge of the big wood in Uncle Huw's car; how else could they have carried the hamper and all the things they had? And then they had gone in single file through the wood, each carrying some basket or rug or other cumbersome object that should never have been brought on a picnic. There were just the five of them. Edward didn't do everything with them, after all. And no Matthew. The woods were dark and deep. The husks of bluebells, moss and cobwebs and dry bark and leaves littered the ground and there was a path forged through the undergrowth by badgers, through the brambles starred with green, embryonic blackberries. But that part of the memory was hazy and brief. What she remembered more clearly was the moment they emerged into the light into a brackeny, rocky field, the castle behind them and the elephant hill before them. They had found a rock that looked like a table and wondered if other people had used it for picnics in the past. She and David and Uncle Huw and Auntie Maggie had waited by it as Phyllis, left behind as usual, came into view, a flutter of moving colour through the trees. There were sheep all around and gorse and buzzards and brightness. There was blue sky and there were white clouds that calmly blew across it.

It all started when Uncle Huw said that he had asked Auntie Maggie to marry him on a day much like that one. A perfect summer's day.

'Did you go down on one knee?' Eira had said.

'I most certainly did. It was in the garden of her parents' house. Auntie Maggie lived on a farm not so far from Priestmeadow at that time and we were walking in the garden and picking strawberries of all things, so it must have been in June, not August, but the point is the day, the weather, was very much like today. A summer's day . . .' and then he broke off and his voice changed. He said, 'You know, Maggie, Lettie Pryce is nothing to me. I never knew what love was until I met you. There was only ever you.' They had looked at each other and held their gnarled old hands.

'Huw. You are an impossible man.'

They were both crying. Eira had watched them, fascinated. Her parents had never cried in those days. David was standing a few yards away calling to Stella, so it was just her and Phyllis on the rug and she had wanted to catch Phyllis's eyes but she was looking away. Uncle Huw and Auntie Maggie didn't seem to mind that they had said these words in front of anyone, in fact they seemed glad.

'Love is the only thing,' Uncle Huw said. 'Remember that, girls.' He blew his nose messily. Then he got up and threw a stick for Stella and made a big show of calling her and going and getting it because she couldn't see it herself and hurling it into the air again, then flinging it to David so he could throw it. Auntie Maggie had started getting out the picnic.

'Come on, girls, tuck in. David! Come and get it!'

Eira didn't remember how they got back or much about what they ate or what else happened. They had probably played in the castle. All she remembered was that she had cast some stupid spell from a herb book and that she had been stupidly happy that Uncle Huw didn't love Lettie after all. She thought her spell had come true. It didn't occur to her, not quite then, that you could love two people. That you could never be sure which one you loved more than the other, or if you were just more used to one person, or if it were possible to love another person at all after your first real love. All those things she had thought so much about since.

CHAPTER 20

Maude is sitting in her wicker chair and I am curled up at her feet on my cushion with Tabitha Twitchett in my arms. The scent of the cut grass surrounds us. We have been tending to the bees and there is some leftover fear still buzzing inside me. Maude is building up to her story again. She doesn't want to waffle and spoil it or rush it when she knows its pace should be slow. She lifts off her beekeeping veil and begins: 'She was only the under-cook, which meant she had all the horrible jobs: scrubbing grease off pots, cleaning the blood from the knives and the boards where the meat was prepared, killing the chickens, washing earth from vegetables in icy water that hurt her hands. And all the time the stable lad pestered her and made his lewd remarks.'

'The one who smelt of horses and hay?'

'He was just an ordinary boy.'

Maude only picks up certain threads of her story when she wants. She snips off or ties a knot in others before they ravel out of control. She goes into the cottage to make the tea.

'But William looked at her as though he wanted to possess her.' Maude crosses her hands over her throat and breathes in. 'And Mary looked at herself in a sliver of broken mirror in the room she shared with Jenny Meredith, the under-dairymaid, and dared to think herself beautiful. Was she beautiful? The answer was yes. She was. And would have been considered so today.'

'As beautiful as Phyllis?'

Maude considers a while and takes a sip of her tea. 'Different.' She puts down her cup and saucer carefully on the little stool we have brought outside with us. 'The cook saw that Mary had caught William's attention. When Jenny Meredith had taken Mary up to their room, before she set her to work that very first morning, the cook had said to the other servants, "That one will cause trouble!" Although, at first, she did no such thing. She worked hard, she liked to laugh – she was only a girl, you see. Just a girl. Not much experience of the world. Only of the little hamlet where she grew up and of helping to look after her brothers and sisters. The other maids liked her company. She didn't have ideas above her station – although, I suppose, eventually she did. William caused that. She had a little red ribbon that she tied in her hair, a way of arranging her clothes. She liked a pretty snippet of lace or anything with a bit of colour in it. But that was all. Only the cook thought she was too beautiful. "I hope you do not come to harm, Mary Evans," she said to herself.

'William could not sleep for thinking about her. At night, the moon woke him. He wanted to touch her just as she had wanted to touch him. He had not known a woman. He decided that she would be his first.'

We stare across the garden, at two cabbage whites, tumbling through the air above the lavender bush. Maude does not change her story because I am a child. She tells it how she thinks of it in her own mind.

'In winter, it can be so dark that anything can happen. It was Christmas, remember. He found her in a deserted corridor between rooms with closed doors and sounds behind them of people laughing and clinking glasses. The flame of his candle danced in her eyes. There was a smell of burning. He looked at her, stared at her until she knew his meaning. Then he hurried away. She did not dare to think that it could be true. She carried on with her work.

'At midnight he knocked on her door. The other bed stirred. "What's that?" said Jenny Meredith. "Only a branch tapping on the window-pane," said Mary. She was lying in the moonlight, her eyes shining. Jenny grumbled and put her pillow over her head. Mary got up and opened the door and closed it behind her, all without a sound. He was waiting. He gathered her in his arms where they stood. All in the dark. She felt the skin of his face against her face, the touch that she could only imagine before. Then her little rough hand was inside his and he was pulling her, like a wind, in her nightgown, like a wind pulling a boat with a billowing sail out onto the sea of sloping corridors lit by the moon. And they lay in the bed together all night, in each other's arms.

'The next day, the thoughts they carried around in their chests were like burning. William Cadwallader had thought that touching her would make him better, but it had not. He wanted her near him all the time. It was intolerable. But she was only the under-cook. "I must go to London," he told his father. Mary heard his horse, clattering out of the yard. She saw the icy puddles he had smashed like mirrors. As soon as he had gone, the stable boy came to her and dragged her by the hair up to the hayloft and forced himself on her and said she was a whore.'

We stay silent for a while. It is very still in the garden, as it was when the story had begun. At times like this, I am afraid of Maude. I do not ask her to explain anything in the story, like what a whore is. I take the story as it is given to me. Maude does not believe there is one way of talking to children and one way of talking to grown-ups. She takes me to the edge of what I can imagine but no further.

I don't feel like going home. I go for a walk, a meandering walk, through fields and hotness and flies, along lanes of tired green leaves, and I end up in the big wood. The trees are huge and wrinkled and ancient and I am small and young and I don't know what will happen to me. The big wood is a sort of lovers' wood. There are trees with initials and hearts carved into their summer dry bark in other summers gone by, splitting open with the heat, and with age, distorting into ugly shapes. One of the oaks has lost a branch and it splices down through the wood like a drawbridge. I walk up it and it leads me up to another branch sticking out and then I reach another until I am up high among the green, threshing leaves. The part where the branch joins the trunk of the tree is so wide I can balance there with my back against the main trunk and my legs dangling down on either side. I can't believe I'm this high.

I peer down, but that makes me feel giddy, so I look out across a very small glade in the middle of the wood. It's all covered in bracken and rosebay willow herb. The only thing about being halfway up a tree is what do you do when you get there? It's a good place for bird watching. I wish I had brought the binoculars. An upside down nuthatch is foraging for insects; a blackbird is singing so close I could touch him. And now I think I can hear an animal; there is a small disturbance of rosebay willow herb, which makes me think there might be an animal there. A hare? I stay very still, my eyes fixed on the spot, and then what rises out of the pink flowers and feathery green leaves takes me completely by surprise.

It's Phyllis, her skin the same colour as the earth, her black hair falling down her back. Her back is arching. But then I see hands, white hands moving like crabs, twisting the folds of her red dress as she bends and rises up again. A sound is coming into the wood from the clearing, like a bird in a trap. She's struggling, gasping, crying out in fear. I'm sliding down from the tree, down the sloping branch, tearing my clothes, my skin, and I land at the bottom, cutting my knee on a sharp rock. Laughter. I stop. Laughter again, the bend of her neck among the feathers of green, Phyllis's laughter and then a male sound that has no words in it. I run. I run back, out through the dark wood, on through the dark wood, stumbling and falling on roots and being scratched by brambles. I run out, past Lettie Pryce in her house, her shadow moving through her room of coloured ornaments, past Maude's cottage. Please, please, don't let her see me. Now she seems foolish in her big hat, her oversized dress, fumbling in her garden with her trug and secateurs, with her stories of people who are long dead and don't matter any more and her snip, snip, snips. I run into the garden. David has seen me running down the lane from the tree-house.

'What on earth is wrong?'

He's there in front of me, his face shocked, blocking my way. I run past him into the house and into Auntie Maggie's apron. 'I've had a fright, I had a fright,' I keep saying. I have to think of something it might be, something not to do with Phyllis. I saw a ghost. I tell them I saw a ghost in the castle. I saw a ghost walking along the battlements. 'No, no, no,' they say, 'don't be afraid. Of course you didn't – you've had too much sun today.' Auntie Maggie fills a bowl with water and Dettol and it goes cloudy and white and she gets out her plasters and she brushes my hair with her ivory-handled brush and David picks out all the little twigs and bits of leaf and spiders and then I start to cry.

At tea time, David says, 'Eira saw a ghost,' and Auntie Maggie says, 'Hush, David,' and Phyllis raises a slim eyebrow over one beautiful, dark brown eye. She goes to bed early to read. I stay downstairs and seem to be watching television but all the time a picture of her keeps flashing into my mind, her back, with the white hands laddering up and down it, her hair splashing down her back, and a human sound that I have heard for the first time.

CHAPTER 21

Every day, Eira resolved to take action about Henry Lux. I will send him a mysterious note, she thought, telling him to meet me at a given location and then I will tell him. I know we are alone in the museum, but it would never be possible there. A London landmark, perhaps, would be best. She watched the shadow of the London Eye turning palely, blindly, in the mist, far away in the middle of London. She thought of certain bridges over the Thames, of the olive-green water rocking below into which they would stare deeply as she made her confession. Or there was the Serpentine – a boat in the middle of the Serpentine where no one could hear her. Or maybe one day in the museum would be better, after all. I will make it possible, she thought. I will choose a day. I will put the closed sign on the museum door. I will go into his office and remove my glasses and dive my hands into his beautiful black hair and say, 'Kiss me, Henry Lux.' And her kiss would put a spell on him and he would forget all about Daisy Lux. Because he did not love her, not really. 'You have wanted to kiss me ever since we met,' she would tell him. 'I can feel it, even here. Here, in the heart of the museum, and so can you. After the party, you wanted to kiss me when Daisy had gone to bed and we were alone in the hall. Kiss me now.'

Then, Daisy Lux went to Glyndebourne for a week. Eira sang for joy as she went about her work in the museum. Henry Lux took to going home the short way. He did not meander through the soft evening light of the park and smell the sweetness of the wallflowers or look into the aviary at the doves while holding hands with Daisy Lux or press a stalk of rosemary between his fingers. He went straight home and made garlic soup, judging by the smell of him the next morning. But nothing happened. All that week, Eira too went directly home, via the off-licence. She sat in her tower sipping wine, listening to Nina Simone, rolling her own liquorice paper cigarettes in a special machine she had found in a junk shop, or curled up on her window-sill, losing track of herself, yet managing not to fall. Not quite yet. On the fourth evening, she got bored with the window-sill and went for a walk because the days were long now and the park was staying open later. She walked between the ornamental flowerbeds, feeling like a ghost of herself, a host of all spinster ghosts, and she felt that Phyllis was there, in the bars of sun that shook on the lake, in the songs of the birds, in the flowers she brushed by. And she kept on, until she was walking down the street of Henry

143

Lux, and she kept on passing the houses, one by one, until she was standing outside the house that Henry Lux lived in, and the light was on. She thought, the light is on. She hovered outside. 'The light is on, so he is at home,' she repeated to herself, perching on the wall. She had tucked a flower behind her ear, a pink gerbera she'd found fallen on the ground outside the florist's. She was thinking of Tahiti. How pretty that moth was, banging itself against the window! Her head was spinning and the flowers in the garden were very white and very luminous in the twilight. A beautiful black cat slid down the bonnet of a car towards her, wanting to be caressed. She brought him up against her bare neck and kissed him. He smelt of dust. She decided to wait there for a while. She thought of Henry inside and wondered if he might be going to bed now and if he would come and draw the curtains. She cowered in the dark. She heard a voice.

'Eira?'

She didn't answer. She put her hands over her face.

'Eira? What are you doing?' She didn't answer. No words suggested themselves, as usual, in his presence. He had a white plastic bag in his hand. He looked at her strangely, as if he were about to ask if she was all right. Then he smiled and said, 'Glass of plonk?' He held up his bag and the wine bottles chuckled inside it. She nodded and followed him in. As they crossed the threshold, the flower fell out of her hair and he trod on it and crushed it. She picked it up carefully, twisting the bruised petals in her hand, trying to revive them. He kept on walking, through the sitting room and on, out into the garden, to the garden chairs. He told her to put some music on, so she went and stared at the CDs, but their titles kept going out of focus and then she picked out the letters of Nina Simone and put her on and came back out and he gave her wine, so she kept on drinking. And when she crossed a certain point of drunkenness, she began to speak. She couldn't remember afterwards, the next day, what she had said. Perhaps, she had told him about her love for Jack and how he drank so much that after seven years she had to abandon him and then he died. Which was not true, because he had not died. Or perhaps she had told him about Phyllis. Or about anything. She could have talked about any number of things.

Now, at this moment, all she knew was that she had Henry Lux where she wanted him, and it had happened just in time, that she would put a spell on him because he was hers. *'Don't take all night to tell me that you love me,'* she sang quietly along with Nina. At a certain point, perhaps when it was very late, and it was just black and cold outside and not so lovely in the garden, he had pulled her up from where she seemed to be lying on the sofa and said, 'Eira, I'm going to take you home, okay?' And he was talking at her as if he thought she was hard of hearing or of unsound mind and she had played along with this idea and they had walked round the outside edge of the locked park, him steering her and her falling against him and stumbling and him stumbling – because, as she thought later, of course, he was very drunk too. And they had looked at the moon and the brown-hazed stars and the moths in the streetlights among the leaves of a horse chestnut tree and smelt lilac flowers in the dark and seen an urban fox, but not a badger or a tawny owl. The journey had seemed to go on for years and years until they were very old, an old married couple who had nothing left to prove to one another at all.

They got up to the tower, in the end, to Eira's octagonal room. There had appeared to be a question of Eira not being able to make it on her own. It had seemed that the stairs were a quite difficult rock face, which they eventually climbed together, and then they got inside and sat on the bed, because she only had one room and the bed was the only place you could sit down, and she had put her arms around his neck in the middle of the spinning, singing room. And there was no need to ask Henry Lux to kiss her. Then they had lain down on the bed in each other's arms and fallen asleep instantly.

Because in the morning he was still there in her arms and they still had all their clothes on. They stayed holding each other. She had a headache. She put her hand on his stomach and stroked a piece of his skin where his shirt had come undone. Then he stroked the hair away from her forehead and said, 'Eira, I am married and I love my wife.' She turned away from him and her tears slid out of her eyes where he couldn't see them. He said, 'If I had met you before. If.' And she had not replied. In the silence they listened to the birds singing outside the window and she realised it was probably very early in the morning, only just dawn, but that he was going to go soon and this would be the first and last time that this was going to happen. She turned over so she was flat on her back and the tears changed their course straight down the sides of her temples and over the obstacle course of her ears and trickled through her hair and sank into the pillow. He was still looking at her and stroking her. He spread out her hair upon the pillow, like wings. He said, 'Daisy is pregnant.' Eira curled away from him again in a tight ball and he got up and left without a word and then she got up and vomited into the toilet. She spent the day lying in the same position, like a corpse, drinking water and sleeping a terrible, deathly sleep in which she dreamed she never set foot in the world again. In the afternoon, it lashed with rain and the windows juddered in their frames and she felt even worse, so she lay down on the floor, because the bed felt too high, and groaned and retched and bit her arms until they were covered in round bruises and the marks of her teeth.

The next day, she didn't go to the museum. She didn't phone Henry Lux to say she was ill. She thought, the thing is that he loves Daisy Lux. He loves Daisy Lux and they are going to have a baby. But the day after that she did go to the museum, wearing long sleeves to cover her bruises, and it was all solved by being very polite. All she had to do was to pretend to be very pleased. It was as if they were ordering her to do this. They made her have no choice. And she knew that this would just go on and on and on and that the baby would be born and that the baby would be a beautiful little girl.

Soon, too soon, she had to meet Daisy in the French café and to hear that the scan had said it was a little girl, which was just what they had always wanted. She had no choice but to go on and on being happy for them and not considering how she might have been the mother of Henry Lux's child instead of being the mother of no children. If. If he had met her before. So it was never mentioned and a froideur developed between her and Henry, which wasn't a real, true coldness, but it was the only climate in which they could both still go on working in the museum, in which they could both still exist. The baby would be born in late summer. Daisy's knitting could be got out of drawers and finished off in time for the first frosts. Eira thought, at least I know. Perhaps now I can move on after all. But she didn't move on. She stayed in a black and terrible cave of despair. And she was frightened of the dark. And all around her it was summer, and the world was more beautiful than it had ever been.

CHAPTER 22

I am thinking again about the night of the moth watch when we had all gone to bed. There is a full moon. The curtains of the window above Phyllis's bed are wide open and the room is bluey-light. She is kneeling on her bed, still dressed, with her elbows on the window-sill, like a portrait of a girl looking the wrong way. I think her hair is where the night is. The black of night. The moon-light looks like smoke coming through the moth holes in the printed flowers of the curtains at the other window and on the carpet of dust where the lead animals of the farm lie out too late. I dare not move. A box of tin trains are tangled in the worst crash of all time. The rasp of David's breathing in the top bunk pulls my eyes up to the roof of rusty metal springs and the ever-falling dust from the under-blanket gets into them and scratches around, just as it does when it gets inside David's lungs. She does not move, even when the grandfather clock chimes one. Uncle Huw and Auntie Maggie and Stella are long ago asleep, Midnight is out hunting, and the house is completely silent. What can she be looking at all this time? I try to imagine her moonlit view across the lawn and over the top of the gingko tree towards the church tower. Roof tops, chimneys, trees full of silver leaves, the sleeping elephant hill. Then her bed creaks and she comes to life. I shut my eyes, quick. When I open them, she is there undressing and that's when I see. It is only for a minute. Her hands slide down her body, pause at her stomach, and then go up to her breasts. She holds her breasts. That's all. Then she puts her arms into her nightie and pulls it down over her head, flicking her hair up out of the top, a black wave falling onto her white back in the moonlight. I've got pins and needles but I dare not move. The plume of fear comes again. David coughs in his sleep and Phyllis looks across at the top bunk but not at me down on the bottom. She does not look at me. Then she gets into the bed and lies facing the window under her pink shiny counterpane. I wonder what her face is doing, as it looks at the moon's. Only now do I realise what I had seen.

CHAPTER 23

Mary Evans wound a little red ribbon round her finger, stirred her tears into the porridge with a long wooden spoon, crouched behind the hen house to be sick over the frosty grass. Maude said that if William had only said goodbye, Mary would have been able to bear it. Mary wasn't stupid. She knew the baby could either be the stable boy's or it could be William's. If it was William's, she could not wait until it was born. But if it was the stable boy's baby, she wanted to rip it out of her insides.

Mary thought about these things for three days and then she locked the thoughts away as though she was shutting the meat safe and carried on as if nothing was happening. If the thoughts tried to come back, she cut herself deliberately with a knife or she scalded herself as a punishment. The style of dresses in those days made it possible to hide a pregnancy, but she wasn't hiding it exactly, she was just not allowing it to be. Everyone had noticed that William had taken a fancy to her. They all laughed about it in the servants' hall, but if Jenny Meredith had noticed that Mary Evans had left their room that Christmas night, she didn't say anything. And still the stable boy dragged her up to the hayloft, whenever he was drunk. And still there was nothing Mary could do to stop him. 'Part of her became hardened by what had happened,' Maude said, 'and part of her was weakened.'

The other servants stopped liking Mary as much as before and they teased her for mooning about. He wasn't even gone that long, just a few weeks. But he did come back. She was in the kitchen garden, because she had crept away when she should have been skinning rabbits, and she wasn't even thinking about him at all. She was thinking how she was never allowed to visit her family any more because she was always so slow in her work now. But she knew her mother would guess what had happened, so perhaps it was for the best that she didn't go home.

When she saw him she started, but he only smiled and beckoned her out of the door of the kitchen garden and then he took off his hat and kissed her. But he didn't want to talk about what had happened when they had lain together that night in his bed and though he kissed her sometimes over the next few weeks and months, when there was no one to see, she knew that he had come to a decision and the decision was not to love her as much as before.

'She couldn't tell him about the baby inside her, any more than she could tell herself that it was there all the time, growing,' Maude said. 'Sometimes the daughters of wealthy families that William's father wanted him to marry came up the long drive in carriages. She wanted to spit in their faces, to cut them with a kitchen knife. And sometimes she saw William look at her, like the very first day. It was summer by then and the days were light so long it was easier to wander away into the fields and for William to forget about his decision. Mary had an afternoon off to visit her family but she didn't visit her family. She went walking by the river with William and, hidden by the tall grasses, they lay down and kissed. Two swans flew above the river like angels and the sun came down on them and William's love began to run away with him a second time. And it was that day that she told him she was pregnant. Couldn't he see? Hadn't he guessed? He stood up. He looked down at her. He told her he was going to be married. "What is her name?" said Mary, but William wouldn't answer. She asked again and he wouldn't answer and she wept and wept because all she wanted to know was a name. This one small thing. "Is the child mine, Mary?" he said. And, because she was angry with him, she said it was not. "Only say it is mine, Mary, and I will provide for the child. Only say it is mine," he said. But she did not answer, and she kept crying. He hated to see her cry, so he strode away through the corn.

'There were those who had guessed she was pregnant,' Maude said. 'They had guessed, though

154

they didn't let on. And, although it was not so frowned on if a woman had a baby out of wedlock in those days, and it even improved your marriage prospects, there was no way that Mary or her family could provide for another child. The stable boy said he knew a woman who had a recipe of herbs and if she drank the concoction, the child would be born dead. He said that he would find the woman. But what if it was William's child? Mary didn't know what to do. She would not take the herbs. She wanted to see the child. She thought, if I see the child, then I will know what to do. She thought that whatever happened, William's love would save her. But she was wrong.'

Maude stopped talking. All this while, the rain had been coming. It was time for me to go. She bundled me out of the door, shoving a broken umbrella at me to make do with if there was a big downpour. By the time I got to the lane, the rain did start to fall heavily and I put it up. In the lane, there was a wet woman in a gaudy summer dress. Lettie. I took a deep breath but when I got closer I saw that she wasn't even going to stop. The lane has lots of little rocks in it, so she kept tripping up because her white sandals weren't very suitable for running. She was far too old to run in that fancy footwear. She didn't even look at me, but she was crying, quite loudly, like a toddler, as if she was only crying because she was getting all wet. When I got back, the house was dark and

Uncle Huw and David were playing turning over cards with just the lamps on, the cards flipping and flapping like pairs of batting wings. Auntie Maggie was in the kitchen, making stock, and Phyllis was in her room.

'Has anyone called?' I said.

'That Lettice woman came to the door. Ridiculous name, Lettice.' Auntie Maggie found a lid for her saucepan and banged it on. 'She had a perfectly good husband for fifty years.' She gave the lid another bang. 'I'll give her old flame.'

I kissed Auntie Maggie's lovely, rosemary-smelling hair and went upstairs to our bedroom and sat on Phyllis's bed. She was curled up, half sleeping, half thinking.

'Phyllis. You have to tell someone.' She didn't move. Then she opened her eyes and stared into mine for a long time. 'Someone like me. You could tell me.'

CHAPTER 24

Where Eira had once looked out at bare twigs, now she saw leaves, so many soft, green leaves, their shaking restless life. For several black days that could have been weeks, she absorbed the fact of the Lux baby. This was the life that the tree had promised in the spring. In the park, there were more couples holding hands, more fat little babies, more families entering through the park's iron gates. She could not compete with Daisy Lux now. Or with any of this. She tried to think about what was real, to remember what had actually happened. How she had even come to be living in her octagonal tower, alone and childless at thirty-six, making up a love story about Henry Lux.

She watched night fall behind the plane tree. In the black wake of Henry Lux's rejection, she let herself think about Jack again and knew he was her one true loss. Handsome, sprawled-in-a-bed-Jack, whose pores breathed alcohol, whose body gently shook as though from some far away child-hood earthquake. Henry was a story, but Jack was real. If Jack knew someone loved him, he tried to love them back. As much as he could. As long as they understood that he had drinking on the brain. Still, now, to this day, at any moment of the day or the night, on any day of the year, in any year that they were both still alive, for ever and ever, she could go to his house, wherever that house might be, and he would open the door and he would put his arms around her and she would breathe in the smell of his body and she would be safe.

In the last days before she left, their flat had been infested with tiny moths. Through all their arguments, the moths had fluttered and swirled about, among the smashed crockery, settling on the edges of the dents the crockery had made in the walls. The fireplace had been cold and empty but the moths had flickered in it where there should have been flames. They had issued, dazed, from the pages of books as they argued about who they belonged to. Eira had killed the moths, slapping them in between her hands until her palms stung. Jack never killed them. All the time they argued, their words flaring amongst the moths, it was about one thing and one thing only. He never raised a finger to the moths. But if only Jack would stop drinking, then they could have a child.

'*If* we have a baby, *then* I will stop drinking.' He blew a moth from her hair, gently.

'I think you will not and that you will drop the baby on its head. I think that you will be unconscious in the night and not hear the baby

158

crying. I think you will hurt my baby by mistake. That you will not be there for my baby.'

'Eira, I cannot do this the way you want. I cannot be the man you want.' He looked at her with his big blue eyes and he said, 'Eira, I can't stop drinking. You might as well ask for the moon.'

She left. Her hair began to turn white; she could not eat; she got so thin none of her clothes fitted her; she lost her voice. She moved to her tower. He stayed in the flat of moths. She dreamed repeatedly of washing him in a bath. She didn't know why she had this dream or why she wanted to do this so much. She wanted to soap every inch of his body. She knew his body off by heart – the bump in his breast bone; the pattern of hairs on his chest; the precise scattering of his moles; the exact creases he had made in his face from smiling; the length of his eyebrows; the thickness of his arms; the flecks in his irises; the shape of his hairline; the smell of his hair; the feel of his penis against her lips. In the dream, she soaped him and then she rinsed him clean, with jugs of clear, fresh water, as if he were a child. She loved this child that he was once, that she could never reach, that she could never find. She had never washed him in her life. They had never even shared a bath. If she had tried to wash him, he would have told her, 'I am dirty and you can't make me clean. I will always be drunk and covered in paint. You knew that when I met you. You knew it all.' But he wasn't always drunk.

Not when he woke up in the morning. Not when he was a child.

The last time she saw him it was Halloween, Diwali and the day the clocks went back. She never thought of Henry Lux then; he was yet to come to her attention. She never thought of anyone but Jack. She pined for him. She had heard his cough on the pavement outside her tower. She had heard him and she had run down, coat on, hat on, opened the door. When she saw him, she knew she still loved him. She saw him thinking that he still loved her. This is what always happened. She saw him thinking that he would touch her but he did not. She knew his thoughts. She knew his touches. Now there was another woman who knew them too.

'It's not like it was with us, is it?' she asked.

'Nothing is ever like us,' he said.

It was the death of autumn. She had spent the day gouging out the brains of pumpkins. Rows of pumpkins lined the streets on window-sills, their pumpkin eyes blazing, silently gloating at what they wrongly thought was the death of love. She and Jack were like one beast, clutching at each other's coats, linking arms into one terrible hulking figure because neither of them could ever let go. They walked for an hour, the last hour before the close of the park, walking quickly in the falling dark. Fireworks ripped open the sky then died. She was still trying to tell him how much she wanted a baby.

'Stop,' he said. 'A robin.' She looked and saw the robin singing as though he were trying to halt the dark. Canada geese took off from the lake.

'Where are they flying?'

'East to Alexandra Palace.' He talked about dying. The doctor had warned him about his heart.

Something was breaking inside her, tearing at her own heart as he spoke. In the dusk, in the Walk, the roses looked dark red, like bloody hearts ripped out. Stars made of yellow leaves fell around them. His eyes were gouged with shadows. He kissed her eyes where they were hurting, said he loved her more than anything, that he always would. She was trying to tell him about wanting his child, only his, because his children belonged to her.

'It is too late.'

'Is it too late?' She wanted to tell him everything before he went away, before the dark. They rushed over the black grass into the unknown of their lives to come. They held each other tight all the way home. When she got inside, she turned out the light in her octagonal room so she could see him waving. Could he see her, or only when the light was on? Slowly waving. She watched as the red lights of the car disappeared, like red eyes, thinking of him crying inside the car.

She fell for Henry because he was there, burning bright in the dark, cold museum, right in front of her nose. Because he was not real. That was how

161

she came to be in her tower, thinking her red thoughts about Daisy Lux. She knew that. Henry Lux had dazzled her. But the love was just a story. She covered her face.

CHAPTER 25

Phyllis would not speak. She could not speak of it.

'Phyllis, I know.' She looked at me with the big, brown eyes. 'Phyl?'

She had hardly taken off her red sun-dress for the last five weeks. People did not look at Phyllis's body, because of the not eating. Their eyes swerved away. She wore the fisherman's jumper over the sun-dress even when it was hot. I could smell her sweat from the end of the bed. I looked at her body now. I thought of touching her.

'You have to tell someone.'

'No.'

'Who else knows?'

'No one.' Not Auntie Maggie nor Uncle Huw. Not David. I could believe that. But whoever was with her in the wood must know. I didn't know who was with her in the wood. I couldn't tell her I'd seen her in the wood. I was too scared. I didn't want to hear that sound in my mind.

'Matthew? Edward?' I whispered. Their names felt funny in my mouth, saying their names. Thinking what I was thinking. She stared at me, then she shook her head and said, 'No one,' again, as if I was deaf. The phone rang. We held our breath. It was Mum and Dad. Auntie Maggie was calling us to go downstairs to the phone so we could all stand round and take the receiver in turn, everyone watching each other's face, straining to hear what was happening on the other side of the world. No one ever used the extension upstairs to listen in. We just always did it like that in a circle. Phyllis answered yes and no and yes and no, winding the cord round and round in her slim, brown fingers and then it was my turn. I said, 'Fine, yes, fine. Looking forward to seeing you too. Bye.' Then Phyllis went back upstairs. I watched her red cheesecloth trail disappear round the banister. I saw the swing behind the moons of the honesty. I went and sat on the swing and closed my eyes. It was one of those summer afternoons when everyone is mowing their lawn at the same time. I thought of Maude. I thought maybe we should tell Maude.

David was back in bed. He had moved bedrooms because his asthma was getting worse and the master bedroom was more comfortable to be ill in. Uncle Huw had been uprooted to the spare room. David was sitting in Uncle Huw's bed with a piece of hardboard on his lap and on the board was a large piece of paper and he was drawing another version of his bird, colouring in the tail feathers, his tongue sticking out. He looked very pale and there were felt-pen marks all over Uncle Huw's sheets.

'Is Master Rabbit at home?' I said, but he didn't answer. 'Are you all right, David?'

'Yep,' he said. I watched him for a while, listening to him wheeze. Dust swarmed over the bed covers in the sun. The hollow at the base of his throat was getting deeper, the lines of his feathers more and more delicate. He looked away from the picture as though someone had suddenly come into the room.

'Is Phyllis quite all right?' he said.

'Yes,' I said. 'Bit too much sun, Auntie Maggie says.'

'She always says that.'

'See you later.'

Uncle Huw was in the study writing in Welsh. He was sucking on his pipe and the room had the lovely smoky smell. I sat and watched him from the sofa, curled up. He didn't mind. I thought he must have been the best teacher in the world. He would have led by example. There was no way on earth I could tell Uncle Huw about Phyllis. He knew about love, I thought, but was this about love? I slipped out of Uncle Huw's study and went back to sit on Phyllis's bed.

'Is this about love?' I said. 'Uncle Huw says it's the only thing.'

'I don't know,' she said.

Auntie Maggie was in the garden weeding.

'I think David ought to go and see the doctor.' I was surprised that I said this.

She said, 'If he gets any worse.'

'He is worse, Auntie Maggie. I don't think the infusion is actually working.'

'Time is the great healer.' She was not un-sympathetic – but her faith in doctors is limited and she wanted to give the magic of herbs a chance to work. Auntie Maggie is seventy-five but she took my mother in when she was my age and later she looked after her when she came home preg-nant with Phyllis. I could have told her. Phyllis could have told her. People always forget what old people know. They think they don't know any-thing. But you are not supposed to know about any of this stuff when you are ten, or only from biology books when you start secondary school. The rule is that you are only allowed to find out about it in biology books. I think grown-ups must just forget what they actually knew when they were ten. The things they knew from using their own eyes and ears.

I decided to go to the library. Maude was talking to a bent-backed man who seemed to have come in asking about books on flower arranging. Maude smiled when she saw me and I went and sat in the children's corner. I found a book on human reproduction. I put it inside the atlas. Inside I saw nine pictures. The stomach wall was invisible so you could see the baby snuggled up inside the womb, getting bigger and bigger in each picture. Phyllis didn't look like the woman in any of the pictures. She didn't even look like a woman. She had managed to keep her baby small like Mary

Evans's by not allowing it to be there. I wondered if I could tell Maude, if I could just tell her and then everything would be solved. When the flower arranging man had gone I nearly said something. But the problem was that Maude did not live in this world, only in the world of stories. Could I tell her this as a story? I looked at the rows of books on all sides. It was too hard.

I went away, back to the house. Phyllis was still lying in bed. Auntie Maggie had brought her a cup of peppermint tea which she had left to get cold so it had a filmy skin on it, like petrol. I asked Phyllis when she thought the baby would be born. She said she didn't know. I went up to the attic to see Edward. I could hear the type-writer going like mad. I knocked on the door and then I opened it.

'Hello, Edward,' I said. He looked disgusted by what he had written on the typewriter. I didn't want to see what it said so I looked away. 'Edward?' Tap, tap, tap-tap. 'Do you love Phyllis?'

He swivelled round. There was a pause in which we both realised that quite a lot of flies had come in from the spinney. We observed them like people at an air show watching all the planes whizzing around.

He said, 'Is it a crime?'

'I don't know, Edward,' I said.

'It's all gone wrong,' he said.

He got up and killed a fly using the method of picking up two paperback books of exactly the same size and bringing them down slowly from opposite sides so the fly doesn't know which way to escape. One of the books was *Live and Let Die*, the other was *Dr No*.

'Yes,' I said. 'Because she's in love with Matthew, isn't she?' I only wanted to see what would happen.

Then he looked straight at me and said, 'Matthew Finn is a decoy. He was supposed to be a decoy.' He looked at me as though he thought he could say anything to me because I was only a child. 'I think, old lady, that she has got into a muddle.'

'No. You are wrong. She is not in a muddle. She told me she is in love with Matthew Finn.' I watched his face. His mouth twitched. 'She wants to get rid of you but she doesn't know how. Honestly, I swear. I'm sorry, Edward. I know you don't mean any harm.' Then I ran away.

I didn't know where Matthew Finn lived, where his farm was where they kept the long boat, but I knew he was always around in the town. I decided to wander about for one hour, asking anyone who was a child if they had seen him. No one had, so I went home and sat in the tree-house. I wondered what Edward would do. After another hour of staring and thinking, I saw Matthew through the binoculars, running along the river path. I rushed down and caught up with him, which was quite difficult.

'Can I talk to you for a minute?' I got my breath

back. Matthew was a boy on the edge of being a man. He lit a cigarette. He was very handsome, more handsome than Edward by far. When the weather was cool, he wore a black leather jacket. I thought: Phyllis loves him and Edward is just getting in the way.

'What do you think of Phyllis?'

'What?' he said.

'Do you love her?'

He laughed. His face was tanned and he had a red T-shirt on. And then he stopped laughing and he took a drag on his cigarette very seriously. He was like a film star. Like Steve McQueen. His eyes looked red, as if too much smoke had got into them.

'Yeah. I do. Yeah.' He walked away. Then he turned and shouted across the field, 'Go and ask her if she loves me!' and he started to run. I watched him running for a long time, red and blue, like a blowing bit of cloth among the yellow ragweed.

By the time I got back, Phyllis was downstairs acting again and I never did ask her who she loved. She was wearing the fisherman's jumper still and I could see that if you were hell-bent on hiding that you were going to have a baby you could do it. Some people wouldn't be able to. But if you thought about it for twenty-four hours a day, if you never, never, never let down your guard. During supper, Uncle Huw read out his Welsh poem and we all clapped, even though we didn't understand a word of it. Auntie Maggie said something in Welsh and Uncle Huw blushed. David had come down as well, but he could hardly eat because he had to concentrate on breathing. I couldn't understand why they didn't take him to the doctor's like Mummy would.

After supper I went and found Phyllis. 'What is going to happen if you just start having a baby one day in the middle of lunch?'

'Go away.'

My last idea was to phone Mum and Dad in secret. I took Auntie Maggie's address book out of her handbag and I found the number that I thought must be the hotel in Fiji because I knew it was called Paradise Palms. I didn't know about things like time differences. I thought if they knew that Phyllis was going to have a baby then they would be glad about being woken up in the night. I waited until everyone had gone to bed, then I crept downstairs to the hall, and I stretched the cord so that I could crouch in the sitting room on the floor and shut the door. Phyllis was asleep. I had no idea how she could sleep but she was asleep. There was a funny tone on the phone like a baby bird. A foreign voice asked me the room number and so I read it out: one hundred and two. Mum picked up the phone. 'Mummy?' My voice echoed down the line, my own voice saying Mummy back to me. I could hear her voice on the other end of the line, talking over the echo. Mummy.

'Eira, is that you? What's the matter, Eira?' I couldn't tell her. I put the phone down and said, 'Please come home, Mummy.' But to thin air. Then the phone rang and Auntie Maggie picked it up upstairs. And then there was a big to-doing and a switching on of lights and I started going upstairs and Auntie Maggie met me halfway.

'You know they're coming home in a week. They can't come any sooner than that, you silly sausage. A week is no time at all!' So no one mentioned Phyllis and I said I was worried about David and Auntie Maggie said she would make an appointment to take him to the doctor if it would make me happy. And she cuddled me in her bed in her cloak of hair until I pretended to go limp so she thought I was asleep, and then she carried me back to bed. I heard her go and check on David and all was quiet.

'Phyllis!' I hissed in the darkness but she didn't answer so I sat up in the bed, not even trying to go to sleep, just leaning against the cold hard wall, waiting for the dawn chorus.

CHAPTER 26

Eira walked away from the museum through the park in the heat, thinking of Phyllis in the cold. Phyllis must have found out she was pregnant in the December of that first year she was at Maldwyn Girls' College, the year before Eira had gone there herself. But Eira knew what it must have been like because she had found out later. She thought of the dark classrooms, festooned with red and green paper chains, of the fake Christmas tree with its winking fairy lights outside the headmistress's study and the papier mâché postbox in the hall for cards. Every morning there would have been hymn practice for the carol service and singing alleluia over and over until everyone got it right. The school play was *Antony and Cleopatra* that year, with Phyllis as Cleopatra, all because Mrs Prince said she looked the part. Eira thought of her sister caught up in it all – the sound of girls laughing on the stairs, the thudding footsteps, like hooves, on the wooden floors, the bells that marked out time. Even now, Eira could hear the scrape of Phyllis's chair as she excused herself from lessons to go and check her pants for blood, praying to bleed, counting the days since her period, a little sum on the edge of her paper as she waited for her turn to translate the next few lines of the Molière. She thought of how Phyllis's breasts must have been hurting, of her hoping that it meant her period was coming, and the first time she felt sick, hiding in the toilets, flushing the chain so no one would hear her retching. All the time, she would have been going over and over her lines for the play, saying them in her sleep, then curtseying on stage and giving Mrs Prince a bouquet of flowers from all the cast, though the standing ovation would have been for her.

Outside, it would have been bitterly cold, but inside the radiators would have got so hot they smelt of burning paint, and all the talk would have been of chilblains and how girls must not sit on the radiators unless they wanted to get piles and the snow would have fallen on the grey crocodile of girls as they walked in single file to the chapel. Eira saw their footmarks in the pure white snow, then, and for all the years to come. '*Unto us a child is born!*' they sang. She thought of Phyllis letting down her black curtain of hair, because it was the end of term and no one would mind, and someone tying some red tinsel in it while she was distracted, staring at the stained glass window with the jagged shapes. Eira thought of Phyllis reading at the carol service, of her having to say 'and they laid him in a manger' without crying, and 'thanks be to God' at the end, and the soloist beginning 'Once in Royal David's City' just as her words died away. It was Phyllis's design that was made into the school Christmas card that year – a picture of the baby Jesus that she'd done in inks in November to be in good time for the printers – and her article about being in the play was in the school magazine. There was only one chemist in Maldwyn, run by an old man called Mr Locke. It smelt of Yardley's soap and respectability and it had a little bell that rang on the door as you entered. You couldn't ask for a pregnancy test there, not unless you were married. Then she would have had to go to the school Christmas dinner at Ashcroft House when the girls had to sit with the teachers. There was a doctor in the town but she could never have gone there, not without telling Matron, not in her school uniform. And, anyway, Phyllis had probably told herself that her periods had stopped like they did before. When she got very thin.

At home, it was a lovely Christmas. Mum and Dad had stopped worrying about Phyllis, because she had put on a bit of weight. Eira remembered that she and David had been still at St Michael's Primary then, making stained glass windows out of coloured tissue paper to stick on the kitchen window at home, happy to open the windows of their advent calendar. They were just writing their letters to Father Christmas at the kitchen table, ready to post to the North Pole, when they all came home from Maldwyn. Her parents had been to see Phyllis in the school play and they had brought her back all shiny-eyed and everyone had said how well she looked now, and that she could easily be a professional actress, but that she should go to university first so she had something to fall back on. Eira had watched Phyllis draw up her revision timetable in red felt pen and stick it on the wall in her bedroom. Phyllis did a lot of work that holiday, when she wasn't lying on her bed reading *Jackie*. Everyone offered to test her but she said, 'No, I can test myself!' and shut herself in her room and drew spidergrams while everyone else watched the *Morecambe and Wise Christmas Special* on television without her. And then it was time for her to go back to Priestmeadow, ready for the new term at school, but as a boarder this time. She must have thought it would be easier to hide her pregnancy at school than at home, easier if she stayed away from Edward and Matthew. Auntie Maggie and Uncle Huw took Phyllis back with them in their car and Eira remembered her waving and sticking out her tongue, and how she had realised how much she was going to miss her. And Phyllis had got good marks for her exams – her mother had read out the list of percentages from Phyllis's letter at breakfast and asked Eira if she would like to go to Maldwyn Girls' College too, and Eira had said yes because she had wanted to follow in her sister's footsteps.

★   ★   ★

When Eira was eighteen, she had an abortion because she didn't want to follow in Phyllis's footsteps. Now, she sat alone in this park and watched white birds taking off from the lake, children playing with boats, an old couple feeding the ducks. It was because of what happened at Priestmeadow. The wind shivered across the water. Because of Phyllis. Eira closed her eyes to shut out the life of the park all around her. She had been on the NHS waiting list for too long because she didn't have enough money to go private and she couldn't tell her parents. She had waited and let the child grow inside her – the child that was going to be killed. She hadn't understood what she was doing. She had still been a child herself. She hadn't understood how she would feel. People had talked about abortions as if they were nothing. She didn't know. She had thought about Phyllis and lied to everyone. It is hard to understand why we do certain things. She hadn't thought that she was allowed to say that she wanted to keep the baby. It was all because of Phyllis. She had never had a general anaesthetic before. She was only a child. She had feared that she might die, that she might never wake up. But she did not die. The child inside her died. She allowed this to happen. The night before the abortion, she had to go to the hospital to have her cervix dilated and they had told her to put her knees together and then to let them fall down at the sides. 'Relax,' they'd said as they put a cold liquid inside her vagina, and then they gave her a rough, green paper towel to wipe herself and told her to come back the next day at eight. She thought, they hate me. She stood in the corridor and waited for the boy who was the child's father. It was high up, that floor of the hospital. If she looked ahead, there was only sky, a darkening, bluish, bruised sort of sky. If she looked down, there were strings of headlights, patches of blackness, a grid of lighted windows on another wing of the hospital. She saw other figures looking out alone but she didn't know what they were thinking, and she didn't know what she was thinking. Maybe he was never going to come. There was no going back now. She rested her forehead on the dirty glass, smelt a fustiness there, and saw the dead flies that lay in piles among the dust. Alone in the corridor, she held her aching breasts, her stomach squeezing itself up at the thought of what she had done. She wanted her baby now, but it was too late. She looked out again, out at the mauve city, knowing her life could never be the same, and her eyes rested on another face looking out from another wing. A tiny face in a wall of light. She couldn't even tell if it was a man or a woman. It was just a human being. All around her in the hospital, at that very moment, human life was beginning and ending. Tomorrow morning, when they sucked the baby out of her, somewhere else in the hospital another baby would be being born. The boy hadn't come, so she had slept in a park. No one came and waved goodbye in the corridor when she returned at eight. It was very dark in that part of the hospital, and she was afraid of the dark. No one was there. He never came. She thought that she would die for her sins. When she woke up, she cried until it was time to go home. When she got home, she cried in secret in the dark. All the blood was leaking out of her. There was nothing to be done. Nothing she could ever do.

'Except to have another child,' Eira whispered to the shadows of the oaks of the park. 'Before it is too late.'

CHAPTER 27

There were plenty of cafés near the museum. There was the café in the park, for instance. But Daisy never wanted to go there. She turned up her nose at it, so they had to drive to the French café. Daisy never mentioned Henry and she never mentioned opera. She always said, 'It's so nice to be ordinary for once, just sitting here with you.' In the presence of Eira, she glowed and preened and shone more brightly, talking loudly, breathing from the diaphragm, about her scan, how she'd looked at the white cloud on the monitor and how magical it was to think that it was really her baby, that she was really going to have a baby at last.

She said, 'Pregnancy makes you tired. You don't know what it's like until you've been through it.'

'Isn't this a lovely cake,' said Eira, glancing at her watch. The one good thing was that they never had much of Eira's lunch hour left before Daisy had to drive her back to the museum, because of the traffic. Because they had come all the way to the French café. Only once had Daisy said something interesting. She had said that

179

when she was standing on some stage in some grand European opera house amid the applause and the bouquets and smiling faces she just felt dead inside because all she wanted was a baby. But all that was past. Now she could live.

She leaned across the table and said, 'How's the love life?' Eira looked into Daisy's shimmery, made-up face. Daisy's breasts strained against their tight, white top. Eira looked away from them, from the massive bulge below them. Every few minutes, Daisy rested her hands on the bulge and rubbed it. Once, she seemed actually to caress the breasts themselves and Eira had been forced to look up at the ceiling. There was a baby screaming out of a red face. Its mother was getting more and more anxious. Daisy looked over and her look was different these days; the way she observed the other woman was new. There was something judgmental now, an exaggerated concern for the baby. Her gaze drifted vaguely back to Eira, back to the question of finding her a man. She did not think that Eira might want a child herself, not until she was married, anyway. Eira was not even at stage one. No one had said to her in her whole life that they loved her more than any other woman in the world and that they wanted to be with her until they were parted only by death. Not even Jack had gone that far.

'How's the love life?' said Daisy again, forgetting she had already said that and then giggling because pregnancy makes you so forgetful. She had already arranged some disastrous dates for Eira, in her busybody way, best forgotten too. Eira thought: my gold standard is Henry. If they are like him, then I will do my best to fall in love with them. But none of them was like him in any way whatsoever. She thought, I must not fall in love with another Jack because I don't want anyone to break my heart again. Someone like Henry would be best. Someone handsome. But these men that Daisy dredged up from God knows where, there were very good reasons why they had no wives.

'I saw you talking to Ray at my party,' Daisy said. Eira had not been aware that Daisy had looked in her direction all evening. They had barely spoken.

'Yes, I did talk to him.'

'I've been talking to Ray.' She frowned. Eira paused. She didn't know if Daisy knew Ray well enough to know she hadn't returned his message, that she had run away from him at Paddington Station. What she hated was Daisy's fat assumption that she should be lucky that anyone at all was even considering going out with her, at her age. 'Beggars can't be choosers,' her big, glossy mouth always seemed on the point of saying.

'I'm not sure if I like him.'

'Rubbish.'

On the drive back to Palmers Green, she started talking about baby names. Eira held her breath and prayed that they wouldn't want to call their baby any of the names that she and Jack had talked

181

about. But, if they do, she thought, there is nothing I can say to stop them. There is nothing I can do about any of this. And when the baby is born, I will have to sit in the French café and watch her breastfeed with her enormous breasts and say how lovely the baby is and all this will be imposed on me unless I put a stop to it. She went inside the cool, black vestibule of the museum, Henry and Daisy frantically blowing kisses to each other over her head.

When she got back from the museum at the end of the day, she phoned Ray and pretended she hadn't ignored his message and that she hadn't run away from him at the station and he pretended she hadn't as well. They agreed to go out for the day on her next Saturday off. He said he'd call her and she knew that he would call her; he wasn't just saying that.

She said, 'Okay, yes, let's go from there.'

CHAPTER 28

I stayed awake all night, sitting on the top bunk bed, leaning against the cold wall. Phyllis went somewhere in the night. She didn't even look at me. To her, I was just a black shape. I watched the hands going round the green dots of her bedside clock until she came back. She was gone fifty-six minutes. She could have been sleep-walking or she could have been sitting downstairs on the sofa reading or she could have been raiding the larder like she used to do when she had the eating problems. What did I know? I heard no sounds to speak of. Then she came back and got into bed and went back to sleep, although maybe she was just pretending to sleep, because I couldn't hear her breathing. Even I, with my lazy eye, could see she was pregnant now. Even in the dark. Auntie Maggie and Uncle Huw had been too busy arguing about Lettie Pryce to see, so that was no wonder. David didn't really look at people's bodies; it wouldn't be something he would consider. I could see that at school you could just wear an enormous jumper all the time; everyone at Maldwyn Girls' College wears their jumpers practically down to their knees, especially sixth-formers, and Phyllis always told me she skived off games. But Edward? Matthew? One of them must know. One of them was the baby's father. As soon as it was light, I began to think about waking her up and forcing her to tell me the truth. I waited for a while, listening to the birds, and then I realised that she was awake already, staring into space. I climbed down and sat on her bed.

'I think you should tell Edward,' I said, just to test her.

'No,' she said, wringing the sheet into a big rope. 'You must promise that you won't tell anyone. Promise? Now go away.'

I promised with my fingers crossed behind my back and then I went downstairs and tried to have my breakfast in a normal way. I tried to imagine Phyllis holding a baby. I tried to imagine the baby she would hold. I thought about how she wouldn't be going back to Maldwyn Girls' College. I would be going on my own now. I tried to see us all standing around Phyllis's hospital bed with the baby in her arms. The problem was that Phyllis didn't even like babies. But I wanted to look after Phyllis's baby if she didn't. I wanted them both to be safe and I wanted Edward to go away.

All that day, Phyllis divided her time between the herb garden and her bed. I sat in David's tree-house on the other side of the garden and tried not to look at Phyllis too much, but just to keep her in the corner of my eye. Lettie called by, all in a blue trouser suit. Uncle Huw answered the door and managed to speak to her for a few minutes before Auntie Maggie rushed out of the covered yard and shooed her away with a broom. Lettie nipped out of the gate just in time but I saw a new light in her face now, a light of mad hope. By lunch time, they had allowed Lettie's visit to whirl up into a tempestuous row. The shouting stage had been while I was in the garden, and some crockery had been smashed. The after-math was during lunch. Now it was all to do with the way they passed the salt and the way they put things down on the table. For Phyllis's sake, I was glad that they were only thinking about them-selves. David was having his lunch on a tray. I took it up to him. It was cauliflower cheese, which he didn't like anyway because he said it tasted of boiled floor cloths when Auntie Maggie made it, and I thought so too. He was asleep sitting up. His felt pens were back in their plastic packet and there was no sign of the bird book or his bird drawing or the board. The room smelt of hyssop. His breathing sounded creaky. I put down the tray and shook him gently. His eyes flickered but he didn't want to wake up. I went downstairs to the phone table in the hall and looked through Auntie Maggie's address book again, all the way through, until I found a name which had Dr in front of it. I dialled the number and a woman answered but I put down the receiver because I didn't know what to say. Then I did it again but this time I said, 'I live at The River House and my brother is very ill. Please come quickly.' Except I didn't. This is what I should have done. Instead, I memorised the number – Priestmeadow 654 – and kept repeating it in my head like a spell, as if I was mad. After lunch, I watched David through the crack in the door. In the end, I lay down next to him and read *The Faraway Tree* aloud. He was only half awake.

All the time, Edward stayed in the attic and Auntie Maggie and Uncle Huw were arguing about Lettie in the sitting room where we were not allowed to go. Phyllis seemed the same. She lay on the swing or on her bed and I was forbidden from speaking to Edward but I told her that at the first sign of anything I would jolly well dial 999. Phyllis didn't answer when I said I was going to dial 999. I stared at the mound under her jumper. I felt like a fly buzzing round a cow's backside. Every so often, she flicked her hair at me to keep me off. Later in the day, Auntie Maggie went for a 'lie-down' and Uncle Huw went to see Lettie to sort things out once and for all. I had planned to go to see Maude because I was supposed to be hearing the rest of the Mary Evans story but I didn't want to leave Phyllis's side. If there was anyone that I could have told about what was happening, it was Maude. She seemed so far away in her garden, though. Her garden was another country, another point in time. How could I ever get to her? But everyone was going to find out about this baby some time. Once the baby was born, Phyllis wouldn't even remember that she had asked me not to tell. She spent most of the rest of the day in the herb garden, swinging to and fro, walking about down there in the big red sun-dress. I watched her from our bedroom. I did not let her out of my sight. I waited to see if Matthew would come to her in her hour of need.

That night, I woke to a commotion. Feet padding along the landing. Talking. Lights and doors. There was a blue light flashing at the window and Phyllis's bed was empty. I ran out onto the landing and saw David in Uncle Huw's arms with a mask on his face; Phyllis, Auntie Maggie and Edward were following in a procession of panicking and there were two ambulance men. One of them winked at me. 'Don't worry, duck. Just giving him a bit of oxygen,' he said. At these moments, you think you might scream or go running towards the person who you think might be about to die. But you don't. You stand back, all sick and shaky. And you don't speak; you go very quiet and you are afraid to go too close in case you get in the way of the ambulance men. You don't get a chance to say goodbye. It was Phyllis who had called the ambulance, apparently. Uncle Huw said, 'Don't worry, Eira, old thing,' and they got in with David. They looked much older than they normally did. I glimpsed David's face beneath the mask. He raised his hand in a solemn wave and the doors slammed and they drove away.

The siren faded. We sat in the snug and drank tea and stroked Midnight and Stella a lot. Edward was dressed half in clothes and half in pyjamas and Phyllis was in the big blue towelling dressing gown that used to be Uncle Huw's. I was in my brown nightie. They told me to go to bed and part of me thought that maybe Phyllis was going to talk to Edward and something important would happen so I agreed. When there was a phone call to say that David's condition had improved, Phyllis came and told me. She kissed me on my forehead. Auntie Maggie and Uncle Huw were staying by David's side.

In the morning, they came back to get some things. They had stopped being angry with each other. Mum and Dad had been phoned. I crept around being quiet, so that Auntie Maggie and Uncle Huw could rest for a while. The house felt like a house that had died. In my mind I flew to Hereford Hospital and landed on David's lips and made his breathing work. It was Edward who rustled up strange, badly cooked meals when Auntie Maggie and Uncle Huw went back to the hospital. There was another phone call to say they wouldn't be coming back that night. 'What if David dies?' I wanted to say. But this is something that you think you will say but, when it comes down to it, you don't, for fear that you will make it happen. Later in the evening, I heard Phyllis being sick, and the sick was green, and it had leaves in it because it was all round the toilet.

I cleaned it up and then I fell asleep. When I woke, it was getting towards morning but the sun hadn't actually come up and there were no birds yet. It was still night; it was just that there was a sense of morning not far off. Phyllis's bed was empty. It is now, I thought. I expected to find her downstairs doing something frightening. Or should I tell Edward? He was the only grown-up. What should I do? I stood stranded, mid-way between the phone and the door to the attic. Perhaps she had just gone for a walk in the garden. I went up and looked out of the landing window and saw a white shape on the lawn in the place where we had done the moth watch. It was Phyllis in her nightie. The front door was open and Stella was stretching, thinking about going outside. I led her by the collar back to the snug and shut the door. Midnight was nowhere to be seen. Edward was not down. I slipped on my Wellingtons.

CHAPTER 29

Eira was inside the London Butterfly House with Ray. A large, speckled brown butterfly was resting, wings closed, on a leaf a few inches from her face. It looked dowdy at first but when it took off it flashed its shimmering blue upper wings and she gasped. Another one circled it. Wherever they looked, butterflies dodged about, some as big as children's hands, with black veins on cream wings, and there were smaller, inky ones everywhere, flying softly in the air, settling and then taking off again. Eira and Ray stood on a bridge over a pond of goldfish in the heat and humidity. A plane roared overhead, enclosing them in its sound. On the other side, obscured by glossy leaves and jasmine flowers, were children exclaiming, talking, asking questions. A fat brown baby came riding by, smiling beneficently like an emperor in a howdah. Eira saw a little girl watching, just as she was watching, in awe. They smiled at each other. In a glass box, all at different stages, hung chrysalises; butterflies were climbing out, unfolding their wings, waiting for their wings to harden. She had never thought that the wings were soft and wet when they were new. One butterfly was resting on the gravel path. She and Ray both saw it at the same time and stepped around it and it flew up between them and settled on Ray's face like a miraculous tattoo. He laughed his loud, deep laugh and it fluttered away and landed on a hibiscus flower. She stared right into its peacock colours. It appeared to have black feathers, black fur, over-laying its wings. They watched smaller ones that seemed to have wings made of glass, sucking up sugar from sponges, and there was the smell of rotten fruit, left there for the butterflies to sup upon with their long thin tongues. They went through the wire door into the aviary where they found the birds her father loved with their startling orange and green feathers and strange, bedraggled songs. Little flocks far from home in a patch of rainforest in London.

It was a good place for a date because there was no need to sit and talk. You could just be together, looking. They wandered around. They sat on a bench inside the butterfly house and their breathing slowed down. She felt less shaky. They had the whole afternoon and then the evening ahead of them. When they had made their way back into central London and walked along the South Bank, they went to Tate Modern because that's where everyone else was going.

'I don't think we have anything in common!' said Ray, smiling. Eira agreed, apart from their obvious shared lepidopterist tendencies. Ray was not handsome like Henry; his face did not break her heart when she looked at it, like Jack's. She liked it. 'You don't seem like someone who should be working in a museum,' he said. They were standing in front of the Giacometti figures.

'Why do I like these funny, thin people so much?' she said. She couldn't ask where he worked or what he did because Daisy had already told her so instead she said, 'What do you write songs *about*?'

'Love,' he said, without smirking or blushing. The word love, said so boldly, so simply. That word. That thing she couldn't get. Because Henry's love was not his to give. Because Jack didn't believe in love any more. Sometimes, she wondered if what she had with Jack was actually love, anyway, or if it was addiction. Was it possible to fall in love with Ray? She changed the subject to what they should do next. He wasn't going to say any more about it, anyway. It was just an answer. Love. He writes about love. So what? In his songs, he writes about love. They had dinner. She felt herself trembling. This is a very good sign, she thought. And then she noticed that his hands were trembling too, quite a lot, as he reached for his glass of water, far more than hers. He saw her looking.

'I'm in recovery,' he said in the same way as he said the word love. They were in the restaurant at the top of the National Portrait Gallery and he looked out and his blue eyes looked even bluer.

'But you were drinking rum and coke at the party.'

'I was drinking coke.'

Eira thought, I am here talking with Ray and he is telling me how bad it got for him. He is just being open. There is nothing he can say that will shock me though, because of Jack. He does not know this. He thinks I am horrified. But I am thinking about how he has done what Jack could never do, how he has made the impossible into the possible. Eira envied the way that he could talk so freely and wished she could tell him about Phyllis, about what happened. In the silence after Ray had finished explaining and they were looking out across London, out across Trafalgar Square and beyond Nelson's Column to the tree-tops of St James's Park and to the Houses of Parliament, she was there with Phyllis again, the last time she saw her. She was in Phyllis's hospital room, sitting on an orange plastic chair with Phyllis lying above her because the bed was too high, and wanting it to be lower so she could see her properly, but at the same time hardly being able to look at her, all wired up like that. She always used to wonder what Phyllis was thinking. But she was probably beyond thinking anything by that stage, only knowing that she must continue what she had begun. Her beauty was lost. She was slipping from the weight of her life. She had never cared for it, not after her seventeenth summer. She just looked weird now, dry and drained, with her big, dead eyes and her strange coating of hair, like feathers, like black fur. For weeks, Eira went to sit by Phyllis, encased in her white bed, the feeding tube feeding her, her big, fishy eyes looking everywhere but at Eira. She was too weak to move anything much but her eyes, so they would just sit there in silence. It was summer and the lawns of the hospital were often being mown. Once, in the days before she hated her, Phyllis had told Eira that her three favourite smells were petrol, cut grass, 'and you, Eira'. But by then she just looked at her blankly, without smiling, like Eira was merely a part of herself, a part of her body that she hated. Her fingers touched Eira's on the bedclothes. I touched you back, Eira thought, your cold fingers, to see what you would do but you did nothing. I laid my white hands on your brown hand and our fingers lay together like woven threads. For a second, your eyes looked straight into mine and I remembered how they used to look at me, in the summer at Priestmeadow, when you were seventeen. You didn't take your hand away. I had to go back to school. I was comforted by the fact that you looked at me and you didn't take your hand away. But you didn't speak. And you did die.

Eira was in the sixth-form common room when Miss Cartwright told her to go to the headmistress's study. She ran past the headmistress's

194

horrible, outstretched arms, up town to Tatty's Tea Room. She sat alone in its doilied silence, then got up without ordering and ran through the streets. She thought she saw Phyllis there, a misty, big-eyed ghost. She lay down among the quaking grass and harebells at the edge of the playing field where Phyllis used to smoke. She ran and ran everywhere, through the invisible body of Phyllis saying the words that Phyllis had never even said: 'It was your fault, Eira. You stupid little idiot. It was your fault.' On the train home to London, Eira sweated and tried to be sick in the stinking toilet but the sick stayed inside her because it was her fault.

She let herself into the silent house. Her parents were standing, dumb, on either side of the fire-place. She remembered the coldness of their hands, their cold skin pressed to her cheek on such a hot day. It was not a shock that Phyllis had died – she had just finally defeated them with her will. And staring out at the boiling afternoon of dust and traffic, at lives not taken, lives that were carrying on however terrible they were or not terrible. A woman came to the door selling dusters and her mother, who never raised her voice, shouted at her to go away and leave them alone. Somewhere, a baby was crying.

CHAPTER 30

By the moonlight, I saw her crouching in the middle of the lawn. The grass smelt wet. For a while, I think, she lay down on the grass. I didn't want her to get cold and wet. I could hear her making a funny noise. We sometimes heard owls crying like that when we were tucked up in bed. Just as I was tip-toeing towards her, she took flight towards the edge of the lawn where it joins the spinney. She didn't look back. I closed the front door softly. The spinney slopes down to the river and there are earth paths with pine needles embedded in them and last year's broken up leaves. My eyes were getting accustomed to the lack of light, but I was following her, like my guide, her moving white shape. You can hear the water at various points where it is fast, but it depends on how high the river is and that night it wasn't very high because we hadn't had any heavy rain. At night, the spinney is dank and dark and deep and full of fear. It's best in the spring or in the early summer when there are bluebells and orchids or even in the autumn when there are interesting fungi, but late summer is dark in the spinney, even by day. I followed her at a distance. She was just a piece of whiteness moving slowly, stopping, then moving on. There is a swing in the spinney, just a normal swing like they have in playgrounds, and she stopped near that. I could see her arms raised, holding onto the chains. I called her because I wanted to get her back, to stop her going deeper. My voice sounded too small for where I was and what was happening. I caught up with her and she turned and I could see the whites of her eyes and her teeth shining. 'Go back,' she said, out of breath, but also very firm, very clear and normal. I knew that I should go back and dial 999, as I had said I would, but I didn't want to leave her all alone. She was this luminous thing, in her nightie, pale blue-white like a giant moth. I realised that she must be making for the old boathouse. She carried on until she got to it and went inside. I heard the door bang, and then she stayed there and there was silence and stillness and a real owl calling and this should have been when I went down and helped her but I was afraid and I couldn't go to her and I couldn't leave. I started to cry. A light appeared, candlelight, flicking inside the boathouse, and I realised that she must have planned this all along. All the time, she had been thinking and planning about going to the boathouse and leaving candles and matches. I stood still, in the dark. It was moving very, very gradually towards morning, although the light was arriving incredibly slowly. Then she came out and she was crawling. I knew I should go to her but I didn't. I just stood there crying for Mum to come home and she went towards the water and she stood up, too near the water, and I thought, what if Phyllis drowns, what if Phyllis drowns, and then she went back into the boathouse and then she came back out and I could hear her noise and she was shaking her hands and I thought I could hear her saying 'Oh, oh, oh' and then she crawled towards some bushes and there was a terrible scream. I ran to her as fast as I could and I knew it meant the baby was being born and I found her lying between the bushes and she was all right but she was being sick and she was soaking and shivering and there was blood all over her nightie. I flapped around her uselessly but she couldn't speak, and there was a small baby all covered in blood and slimy stuff lying on the ground between her legs and we tried to make the baby cry and we shook the baby and smacked the baby but the baby didn't make a sound because it was dead. And I held it and it was a girl. And Phyllis had brought a knife from the kitchen drawer and she cut the umbilical cord, blood all over her hands, and eventually this lump of red came out and I wrapped it in the nightie and dropped it in the river and it was all muddy and I held the bloody, muddy nightie in my hands and Phyllis crawled into the boathouse naked with the dead baby against her and I went to wash the nightie and I couldn't get it clean.

When I went back, she was in the boathouse and the dead baby was lying in a blanket that she had made to be a cradle on her chest and she had put on the fishing jumper, and she was lying in her own green sick. I could smell the blood and the dead baby was all white now and I put my hands round hers and the blood stuck them together as it dried and we made the journey back through the wood very slowly, with the baby in the blanket, and when we got back to the house I thought, *Red sky in the morning, shepherd's warning.* We locked ourselves in the bathroom and got in the bath together and I helped her wash and I rinsed the blood off us, over and over again with Auntie Maggie's enamel jug, and all the time she wouldn't let go of the dead baby, which made it very difficult. She watched me clean the bath and she took the dead baby with her into her own bed and hid her under the bedclothes and I went to get Edward because he was the only grown-up and I didn't know what else to do.

CHAPTER 31

I went up to Edward's room. I went up his stairs and knocked on his door and I called his name. My voice sounded small and dull again, like it had in the spinney. He was always up by now, doing his morning stint on the typewriter. But not today. I got dressed and went downstairs and tried to think about getting breakfast; I wondered if Phyllis could manage a piece of toast. I put the kettle on. I didn't want to leave her very long, even if she had gone to sleep. Downstairs the curtains were still drawn and it was very dark and gloomy without Auntie Maggie there, so I drew the ones in the dining room and then I heard scratching coming from the snug, so I let Stella out and then into the garden, where she started barking like a maniac, which was the last thing I wanted her to do. She'd made a puddle on the floor and I was going to clean it up, except there wasn't any toilet paper left. Midnight was crying for food but I couldn't work the tin opener so I gave her a saucer of milk. I went to the front door. I could see our tracks across the lawn in the dew. Something looked different. Edward's car was gone. I ran back up to the attic. All his things had disappeared and the room was bare again like it used to be. All his poems and his books and his heaps of paper were gone and his typewriter, everything. The window was open, letting blue-bottles come in willy-nilly. I sat down on his bed and tried to work out what had happened. My heart was beating fast. I saw a corner of a piece of paper sticking out from under the bed, an escaped draft. I used to think drafts meant cold winds but Edward told me they were disasters. The paper was blank, except for the indentations of writing from another piece of paper that had been resting on top of it. I ran my fingers over the indentations. I folded it inside my pinafore pocket and went back to Phyllis. She was asleep. She looked a strange, yellowy colour. The dead baby was still underneath the quilt. If she had been awake, I would have told her about Edward. I lifted the quilt up and saw the dead baby. It looked like a waxy doll with a folded-up face. I prayed for a miracle that the baby would come back to life, then I listened to check that Phyllis was still breathing properly.

'Don't die,' I said. I heard the kettle whistling, so I went downstairs and had some cornflakes, then I laid out everything on the table and put milk in the bowls and one or two cornflakes sprinkled in each bowl and orange juice in the glasses. I drank the orange juice to look as though we had all had breakfast as normal and I made some toast under the grill and crumbled the crumbs on the plates and I took the toast up to Phyllis and a cup of tea. She drank the tea but left the toast. She was trying to get warm by holding the cup so I got a hot water bottle from the bathroom and filled it from the hot tap. Neither of us felt like speaking. The baby was still there. Phyllis lay down again and I said, 'Edward's gone.' She turned her face inwards into the pillow. The phone rang. I answered it in Auntie Maggie's bedroom. She said they were all coming home and David was fine. 'Oh, good,' I said. They would be back in an hour. Phyllis gave me a towel soaked in blood and told me to put it in the washing machine, and the nightie, and to turn the dial to one and press it in and to put a capful of bleach in the drum, then she sank back into the pillow. Every time I left the room, I knew she was looking at the baby, hungrily taking her in. When we thought they were nearly back, we decided to put the baby in the drawer of the dressing table next to Phyllis's bed, wrapped in the fishing jumper.

David was back to his normal self. He'd had a chest infection that was clearing up and now he had to take an inhaler and some tablets from a brown glass bottle and he had a badge for being good. I waited to see if he would be coming back to the bunk bed but I saw Auntie Maggie put his tablets on the bedside table in Uncle Huw's room again where he had been before he went to hospital. She took away an un-drunk mug of hyssop tea and poured it down the kitchen sink. I said that Phyllis hadn't been well but now she was feeling better.

'Not another one!' she exclaimed.

'*The curse has come upon me,*' said Phyllis.

'I know just the thing for that,' Auntie Maggie said, gazing out at the herb garden. All the time, the baby was in the drawer. I stood in front of the drawer, whistling a happy tune like in *The King and I* and then I followed Auntie Maggie downstairs. I could hear David and Uncle Huw wondering why Edward had gone out in the car. In the end, I decided to go up to his attic and to pretend to discover that he had gone.

'He's gone, Auntie Maggie,' I said and I started crying but the crying wasn't pretend. She put her arms round me.

'What do you mean gone, my little chickadee?'

They will never be able to explain it. They will never know why he left. He had left his rent in the teapot. There was something I needed to ask Phyllis very badly but now didn't seem the right moment. I had found a green wax crayon in David's art box and I rubbed it over the paper with the indentations on it until some white letters appeared against the green. All it said was 'Darling'.

Once David and Uncle Huw were settled in front of the cricket, and Auntie Maggie was sitting with some knitting, I went to see Maude. I knew

I couldn't be too long because of Phyllis. I wasn't really going to see Maude. I was going to steal a spade from her shed but the shed was locked. The front door was open and I went into her kitchen where she was reading a recipe book with her specs on the end of her nose.

'What's the matter, my little love?' she said over the top of the specs. There was a long, dark silence. Tabitha jumped into my arms. I kissed the tip of her ear and felt a spark. I told Maude everything that had happened, everything I could think of. Maude's specs fell down on their chain. Her face had gone white and she covered it with her hands. I watched and waited by her chair. I didn't know what to do. I knew she was deciding for me. She uncovered her face but it was still white. She took off her apron and fetched her cardigan from the bottom of the stairs and then she told me to go and wait in the car. I saw her getting the spade and she put it in the boot with some other things I couldn't see and slammed the door. We drove up to the big wood and we walked for a while until we found a certain mossy rock under an oak. All the time, Maude was thinking. We were near the glade of rosebay willow herb where I had seen Phyllis that day. Maude dug a hole very deep and I helped when she had to stop for a breather. Maude was very strong and good at digging but by the end she was shaking and there was sweat running down her face. Then we drove back into Priestmeadow and out and down the lane to our house. We sat in the car for what seemed like a very long time with Maude thinking and me waiting. Then she told me to get out of the car and fetch Phyllis out of bed and to tell Auntie Maggie that Maude would like to take us for a picnic.

'Maude would like to take us for a picnic,' I said to them all looking up at me. 'Phyllis and me,' I added, in case David thought that he was coming. Maude came in behind me and I could hear them all chatting brightly while I went upstairs and helped Phyllis to dress and led her out to the car.

'I'll check you over afterwards, my lamb,' Maude said when she saw Phyllis. We drove back to the big wood. We were going to put the baby in a box that was a writing box with a pair of birds carved on it and a brass key that I had seen in Maude's sitting room, but Maude said that perhaps Phyllis would like a few moments to say goodbye. She took me by the hand and we went and sat on a stone and she put her arm round me very tightly. We didn't say anything; we just looked out at the bracken and a woodpecker flew by. When we turned round, Phyllis was still holding the baby and staring at her and it was a long time before she was ready to put her in the box. She told us that the baby's name was Summer and she kissed her head. There wasn't any hair on the baby's head. She sang 'Hush, Little Baby'. She knew all the words. None of it was going to happen. Then she put her in gently and carefully closed the lid and locked it and she held the key in her fist all the time and I wondered what she would do with the key. And then Maude said some of the words from the Christian burial service from a little black book of prayers she had in her pocket and we put all the soil back in. That was when Phyllis started screaming, 'NO, no, no, no, no, no, no!' so we had to dig out the soil and get the box out again and unlock it so Phyllis could look at Summer one last time and kiss her goodbye again. We were all covered in mud now and Maude looked very pale and tired and Phyllis just lay on the ground crying. Maude and I rolled the big mossy rock with all the strength we could muster and it sort of fell over on top of the grave, which was a complete fluke. When we got to Maude's house, Phyllis had a bath with salt in it and I washed the mud off at the kitchen sink and Maude checked her over in her bedroom and she decided that she was all right but she said to ring her up if Phyllis had a temperature. She found us a thermometer and made us some toast, which we couldn't really eat, and then she drove us home. So Summer was buried in the wood. Mum and Dad were coming home in one day's time. And when I had been helping Phyllis to dress, I had seen a letter from Edward under her pillow, pages and pages of black handwriting that began with the words *My darling,* but I never got to find out what the rest of it said because I didn't get a chance to ask before Phyllis stopped speaking to me.

That night, I went and sat on the gatepost. It wouldn't get dark until late. It was nearly our last evening. I sat there alone for a long time, calling for Mum in a low voice, and then I saw Matthew coming up the lane. I knew him by his walk, but he didn't see me. He flung his bike down on the verge and lay on the grass and the bike wheels kept on turning and ticking and turning and ticking.

'Matthew?' I said softly. He thought I was a child who didn't know anything. I can never be a proper child again, now.

For a second, I think he thought that I was her. He lit a cigarette and it seemed that he was going back to the verge but he came up and sat on the gatepost with me.

'I know about everything,' I said.

'About what?' His face was very close and I could see his eyes were pricking with tears. He had been a decoy. But was that all he was? It had been Edward in the wood. And Edward had run away. He had gone away and left her. And if I hadn't told him she loved Matthew he would still be here. He must have thought that Summer wasn't his baby. All because of my acting. All because I wanted to see what would happen.

'If you don't know, I can't tell you,' I said. 'I thought you knew.'

'I hate Edward Fucking Furnace,' he said.

'Why do you say that?' I said, hoping for something that would tell me I had been wrong. But he didn't answer. 'Well, he's gone now,' I said, 'so you needn't worry.'

I knew she was lying in bed. I looked up at our room and saw the light was on but she wasn't there at the window. There was no point in her looking out now. Something in that letter made her sure Edward wasn't coming back. Matthew looked at the front door, which I had left ajar, as though he was thinking of rushing into the house. But I think that he realised that even if he did it would be useless. He could plead with her for ever and she would not breathe a word. Nor ever tell him that she loved him or about Summer. And he was right. He jumped down from the gatepost and on to his bike and cycled away, fag in hand. On to pastures new.

CHAPTER 32

'They're here!' shouts David with his newly working lungs. We come out from our various corners of the house. It's the middle of the afternoon, hot and sleepy. All day we have been waiting. Their plane landed in London this morning, and they've come all this way, straight from plane to car. Here's our old car, reminding me of our old, safe, ordinary life. Uncle Huw and Auntie Maggie are reconciled. They are like butterflies that meet and settle together on the buddleia and then go reeling madly away from each other until they come together again like now. But I wonder if they are really as all right as they seem on the outside. This is becoming something I think about more and more: the difference between outside and inside people. Lettie came to see us this morning. She only got as far as the middle of the drive because Auntie Maggie saw her from where she was hanging out the washing. I was there behind a sheet. Auntie Maggie ran towards her, in that heavy, clumsy way that old people have of running, with a clothes peg in her hand as though she was thinking of clipping it onto Lettie's nose. Lettie backed away in a flap, all done up in a sailor outfit.

She shouted: 'I'm going away on a cruise!'

Auntie Maggie stopped running. The words 'going away' had tripped her up.

'Cruise!' said Lettie.

'When?' said Auntie Maggie.

She said she was going in a week. That it was best. She'd put her bungalow up for sale as well, so we found out later. I wondered if we would end up adopting Tam. She turned, reluctantly, sneaking an eye at the house, thinking that it contained Uncle Huw. He appeared nonchalantly at the gate, back from taking Stella to 'do her jobs', as Auntie Maggie always so unappetisingly said, and approached Lettie's turned back. Auntie Maggie eyed him. I had come to Auntie Maggie's side now. I was holding her hand. Lettie's and Uncle Huw's hands touched in a butterfly touch of their own. I felt something, like an electric force, run through Auntie Maggie as she tried to step forward but I held on to her with all my strength. Then Lettie turned away. I admired the jaunty little angle of her hat, the way she kept her chin tilted up. And I could see that Uncle Huw did too.

But all that had been this morning. Then they had just carried on with their chores – Auntie Maggie preparing lunch in her usual trilling way, Uncle Huw energetically cleaning his golf shoes as though nothing had happened, seeming to accept that Edward had gone, that he had just been a ghostly galleon that had passed us in the night. Back to Swansea University, or Newcastle-upon-Tyne, or wherever he came from in the first place. Phyllis had come down too, like a black cloud, and then gone back upstairs.

Mum and Dad get out of the car looking creased and brown and in love. I see from the landing how they look expectantly up at the house, waiting for the three of us to run out into their arms. But we don't. We stand in the porch, feeling shy in our bare feet, and they come to us. Closer and closer across the cracked tarmac. Dad picks up David, pleased as punch. He is the one. All back to health. Dad holds him tight. I don't know what he'd do if he lost David. Next it's me, because of the phone call, and they know I missed them. I feel my mother's body, my father's body. My throat is hurting as if I am about to cry but I can't seem to cry. I'm afraid that Mum will be able to tell what has happened just by looking at our faces. I look away from her eyes. I don't like having secrets. My inside feels all torn and red. Last of all it is Phyllis's turn. She just looks normal on the outside. Everything that has happened is sealed inside her, safe, even though she's the one with the insides torn and red. I know that she wanted the baby, but also that she didn't.

★　　★　　★

It is nearly time for the new term to start at Maldwyn Girls' College. I have been with my mother to a shop in Hereford to buy my uniform – particular types of socks and a hockey kit and *Hymns Ancient and Modern*. We have been sent a diagram showing the height of sock permitted, the height of heel on shoes that is allowed, which is no more than one and a half inches. Phyl doesn't come because she's got all hers from last year. It seems wrong for Phyllis to be in a school uniform now. Mum and I try to talk in the car. All the time I am thinking she will say something about Phyllis and the game will be up. But she talks of being in a rainforest, of leeches and bird-eating spiders, and there are the names of the birds, and I know what they look like now because I have studied their pictures. The warbler didn't put in an appearance. I tell her about the bird book, about Maude, but I don't say anything about Mary Evans because I haven't heard the end of the story. They haven't seen the warbler yet. Perhaps they will see him when they go back and Daddy starts his job at the university, Mum says. I want to ask her if she and Daddy are really in love or if it is just a look they have. They've found a Fijian school for David. He's full of excitement about going, like a chirrupy warbler himself. When we get home, I lay out my things. I've got a satchel that Uncle Huw has given me. I think the satchel will be too old-fashioned but I can't say anything because

I don't want to hurt his feelings. He gives me some saddle soap to clean it because it's been lying in the garage for years and even the catches are rusty. I think it must have been Mum's satchel when she was a little girl. I clean it and put my bible and my ink pen inside. I won't be seeing London until Christmas. Whenever I go into the bedroom, Phyllis goes out.

We're all having supper when the phone rings. The phone doesn't often ring when we're all here. Phyllis jumps up but Uncle Huw goes out to the hall to answer it. When he comes back, he says that he has some very bad news to tell us. Edward's been in a car crash and he has died. Phyllis's face drains of everything that it contains and then it draws itself up and then it crumples down again. She gets up from the table, dragging the cloth, and plates and knives and forks go crashing to the ground. David catches her glass and almost laughs but puts it back quietly and then Phyllis is not there any more and it's just us in the room and silence, a cabbage white flying out of the lavender under the window.

'I don't know the circumstances,' says Uncle Huw, his voice a whisper. The meal is abandoned and I am running up to the bedroom, to Phyllis, right behind Mum and Dad. And Dad is trying the handle of the door, up and down, up and down, but of course she's locked it. I think of her turning the key, of the key in Summer's coffin with the carved birds. Mum's calling, 'Phyllis,

Phyllis, Phyllis . . . Open the door, open, open, open up.'

And all I can hear is her singing, 'Hush, Little Baby' like when we were in the wood. Don't say a word, I thought.

CHAPTER 33

We packed our trunks to go away to school and Mum packed David's things in her case. He had a supply of inhalers but he probably wouldn't need them because of the climate in Fiji. No one said anything about Edward's funeral. No one said anything about why Edward had a car crash. We didn't know all the details because we weren't family. We realised we didn't know much about Edward or if he even had a family. He seemed as though he was someone who had come to Uncle Huw and Auntie Maggie because he hadn't got one. Apparently, it was all because Uncle Huw had met him on the Aberystwyth train, studying a poem by John Keats called 'Ode to Psyche'. We did the same things we would have done if Edward hadn't died. We didn't stop talking to each other or laughing or having meals. Sometimes, we paused and realised what we were doing. But Phyllis realised all the time. She came down and she took part in things but she wasn't really there because half of her had died with the baby and the other half with Edward. I thought of Matthew and wondered if he would come to comfort her but he was never around.

When Phyllis went for a walk, I looked through all her things, through every single thing she possessed, but I couldn't find the letter. I opened the drawer where I had laid the baby. I didn't find anything, of course. I couldn't bear to look inside that empty drawer. I wished it had a key so it could be locked for ever and no one would ever be able to open it again. And I knew that she hadn't just gone for a walk. I knew that every time she said she was going for a walk she went to the green heart of the wood and lay down on the ground by the rock. When she came home her eyes were swollen and there were tiny pieces of moss in her hair. Once, I tried to pick the moss out but she slapped my hand hard. On the last day, when we were checking the rooms, I found *The Magic of Flowers and Herbs* wedged behind the headboard of her bed. I wanted to take it back to the library but the library was closed, so I kept walking until I got to Maude's house, even though I knew we were leaving in two hours. I hadn't seen her since the day we buried Summer. She was sitting in the wicker chair outside her front door as usual, but she was clutching Tabitha Twitchett. Everything had changed.

'Hello, my dear,' she said, holding out her hand so that Tabitha had to cling on to her cardigan with her claws to stop herself falling. Maude's hand felt cold, even though she had been sitting in the sun.

'Hello,' I said, dodging away from her, and letting go of her fingers more quickly than she wanted me to. I leaned *The Magic of Flowers and Herbs* inside the porch and walked slowly over and sat down on the grass by her feet. I knew we were both thinking that this would have been the time when she would have been telling me the end of the Mary Evans story. I still wanted to hear it. I wasn't sure if it would be all right. Very faintly from the town, I could hear the church clock striking as though this were a perfectly ordinary day.

'What happened to Mary Evans? Why did they hang her?' I asked at last, as I had asked her once before.

Maude didn't answer. She just looked down at me and I noticed that she had deep shadows round her eyes. I felt angry that the story had been interrupted, angry that Phyllis had spoiled our friendship that crossed the generations.

'I think it might be better not to tell the rest of the story, just now,' Maude said. She looked down at me again and I looked up at her and I said that I wanted to hear it, that she couldn't just leave it without an ending. I could feel a big lump in my throat.

'Please tell me,' I said.

So she did tell me. But her voice was different now. There wasn't any life in it and there was the worry for both of us that I would have to go back soon because it was my last day and we didn't

217

have much time. Maude sighed. She said that one day, in late September, Mary Evans said she felt ill and took to her bed in the servants' quarters. Only the cook noticed her take one of the knives from the kitchen. The cook bided her time and made a rabbit pie. She had her suspicions about Mary Evans, but she didn't say anything. She gave instructions that Mary Evans should not be disturbed. At dusk, when the cook knocked on the door, there was only silence. The cook opened the door and found Mary inside, shaking from head to foot, trying to pretend that nothing had happened. The cook pulled back the covers of the bed and saw there had been a hole cut into the mattress and Mary started sobbing as if she were being torn in two. The cook looked into the hole and saw a newborn baby inside, all among the feathers. Maude looked at me, hesitating. 'The baby was dead,' she said.

'Why was the baby dead?' I knew I was saying the words too slowly, as if they were the words of a joke. I was thinking of Summer and being in the spinney, how we had tried to make her breathe in the boathouse. Of Summer's tiny body covered in Phyllis's blood. The knife from the kitchen. The baby in the drawer, in the box, in the earth, in the wood.

Maude stopped the story. 'Eira,' she said. 'Phyllis didn't kill her baby. You know that, don't you?' She paused and tried to touch my hair but I shook her off. 'No one killed Summer. She was born dead. That can happen sometimes.' I couldn't believe that any of this had happened at all. I wanted things to go back to how they had been before. I thought of the green sick in the toilet. I wondered how Maude could have not told anyone what we had done. Why was this secret being kept?

'Why was Mary Evans hanged?' I repeated. 'Was the baby born dead?'

'Mary Evans was hanged because she killed her baby daughter with a kitchen knife,' said Maude quietly. 'She was found guilty of murder and hanged. She told the court in Priestmeadow that she had done it out of mercy for the child. It was thought that the child had died instantly, but the jury said that she had been seduced by the devil and condemned her to death. If Mary had been sure it was William's child, perhaps she would have asked for his help. But she wasn't sure whose child it was and for this she blamed herself.'

'Why did they say on her gravestone that she suffered?' I said in a cold voice.

'She was so young, only sixteen. She didn't know what to do. It was not her fault, everything that happened. She felt she had no choice.' Maude looked away at the crows flying over the garden towards the wood, then back at me with her shadowy eyes. 'One rumour says it was William Cadwallader who put up the gravestone years later, when he was an old, old man, because at first she had no gravestone, being buried in unconsecrated ground. Others say that William

219

Cadwallader and his father served on the jury that condemned her to death. More often than not, these young servant girls who took desperate action like this when they were in Mary's situation were not hanged, and so it might even have been the people of Priestmeadow who paid for the gravestone because they disagreed with the verdict of the court.'

'She didn't have to kill her baby!' I got up and started to walk quickly down the path. Then I stopped and looked back. Maude had her head in her hands. 'I think she deserved to suffer,' I said. My voice had gone croaky. I felt angry and shaky. I wanted to run home but my legs felt too heavy. I stumbled out of the garden without saying goodbye. I wanted to run back and hug Maude but I couldn't. I went past Mary Evans's gravestone and read the words about being without sin. I did not know if I was without sin. Or Phyllis.

CHAPTER 34

That same day, Phyllis and I are sitting opposite each other in a train carriage with just us in it and a door to the outside, which is fields and fields of passing green and scatterings of sheep that look like stones spelling out a clue for me to read and understand if only I wasn't so stupid. It's the Hereford to Maldwyn train, and there are other girls dressed in grey, but we don't mingle with them. Dad had helped us on with our luggage into this carriage and we can't very well leave it. Anyway, there's no one that Phyllis knows on this train and it is not as if I am going to know anyone. We'll manage somehow when we get to the other end. Uncle Huw wanted to know if they still have such things as porters in this day and age. They were all standing there on the platform in a little gang, waiting for the train to go. Edward would have been there, but he was not because he has died and we still don't know, nor does Phyllis, nor does anyone, where he is even being buried or whether his funeral has been or if it is still to come. He has gone out like a light. Mum and Dad and David were all in a three. I didn't like them being all in a three. Auntie Maggie and Uncle Huw were standing on either side. 'Won't be long until Christmas!' Mum said even though it wasn't even autumn yet. We'd already hugged and kissed. Then we were just looking and waiting and sliding away in a big noise. The person who kept waving longest was David. He waved until he disappeared.

When I was little, we went on a fair ride. You had to get into a little carriage and then you set off in a line of carriages up a steep slope and across a rickety bridge – it was very high, but what I didn't realise was that it was only made to look as if it were rickety. It didn't look safe to me and we were all sitting in the carriage and it was just about to start, or maybe it had just started, and I wanted to get out and I actually tried to get out because I was so scared that I thought we were all going to be killed by falling from the rickety bridge. I lunged for the platform edge, hurting Dad's leg in the scramble of him trying to keep me in my seat, trying to stop me from getting hurt. The ride went on and I closed my eyes and we survived and all that happened was that everyone said I was silly for being afraid and that now poor old Daddy had a nasty gash on his leg. I felt like that now. I wanted to get out and run back along the track to where they were all standing. Except they wouldn't be standing there any more. They would have driven away by now, and even if they hadn't they would have just said I was being silly. 'Have I killed Edward?' I wanted to ask.

I watch Phyllis falling into herself. I am the last person to be able to save her. This is going to be our last conversation, a conversation of a handful of words. There isn't a table between us, just the hot air between the seats, the tall seats for adults and the net rack for the hats that no one wears any more and the high mirror for people to look in as they tidy their hair and powder their noses after the journey and the ashtray with criss-crosses on it to stub out their cigarettes. It is so hot and stuffy and dusty. I've got bubble gum in my pocket but I don't dare put it in my mouth because I don't want to look as if I am happy, which I'm not anyway. I am wondering if the blood is still coming out of Phyllis. She looks puffy and she hasn't even brushed her hair and she hasn't put on her kohl eyeliner even though she normally puts on her make-up the moment she wakes up, like in the song. Once, the train just stops. I wonder if the train tracks ahead have completely melted and we will have to reverse back into our old life. The window is down and we can hear a lark. I know we can both hear it because I can see Phyllis's eyes searching the sky but neither of us says anything. We just listen to the lark. When she speaks, the lark is an accompaniment to her words and her eyes are joining the red dots of the poppies. Later on this journey, we will see Michaelmas daisies by the thousand. It is a wonderful year for Michaelmas daisies – all those purple stars. She leans forward. Her voice is quiet.

'I don't know who . . .' Her voice dips. The train starts again in a big noise. 'Matt or Ed. I didn't know. It could have been either.'

I try to answer but I can't. 'He loved me,' she says, and I know by this she means Edward and that it was definitely me who had spoiled everything and that she knew that. And now he was dead. 'He knew about the baby. We didn't know what to do. I didn't want to tell you. You're too young.'

She turns away to the window, to the blue heat and a bank of shocking pink rosebay willow herb. She has started crying, but it sounds like a faint scream, heard from very far away. Some girls are going past down the corridor so I stand up to hide her from their prying eyes.

'Phyl.' I put my arms around her. I brush her face and my knuckle gets tears on it. Her shove sends me across the carriage and back into my place. She does not say it is my fault. She does not say she hates me. Not in words. Is it my fault?

'If you ever breathe another word . . .' She doesn't finish her sentence.

A guard comes in to check our tickets, just in his shirt sleeves but with his hat still on. He doesn't look at Phyllis in the way that men usually look at her, because she is not acting. He looks down on her with his smell of aftershave, his gold chain, the ginger hairs poking out of his shirt at the neck. He winks at me. There is a cream, crusty stain on the flies of his trousers, right at my eye level. He goes to the door and slams it behind him and the jolt goes through Phyllis and the smell of upholstery escapes suddenly, like boxed sick. She doesn't tell me that she is never going to speak to me again. She just stares at the window and then out of the window, then at her reflection, then at the horizon. I couldn't go back to say goodbye to Maude after I ran away. What has happened has spoiled our friendship. Perhaps she will write to me, but she probably won't.

I look out, as Phyl does, back and forth from the window, near and far, far and near. The hills of Wales have disappeared long ago, cut off for ever. I remember Phyl cutting the umbilical cord. I remember washing the knife with Fairy Liquid in the sink and thinking of that advertisement where the little girl says, 'Why are your hands so soft, Mummy?' And putting the knife back into the drawer where it would go to cut cheese and bread. I think of Phyllis's blood swirling round and round in the river, getting caught under the cows' hooves at the weir, particles of Phyllis and Summer whirling and eddying in the water, a king-fisher dipping into the black water to drink.

Phyllis is getting out her make-up, blotting her eyes carefully with a fragment of old tissue. I've got a clean tissue in my pocket but I dare not give it to her in case she hits me. She pulls her eye down and draws a black line over and over the rim of flesh between her eyelashes and her eyeball. She combs her hair, and strands of blue-black hair fly around in the sun, in the dust, particles of Phyllis. She puts on her lipgloss. She gets her tiny stud earrings from her blazer pocket and twiddles them in. I eat my sandwiches because I am hungry and I think that I might as well and if I don't eat them I will feel worse and I don't know how to feel worse than I do already. Phyllis lobs her sandwiches out into a field. Once upon a time, I think, she would have given them to me. She chews the frayed strands of the cuffs of her jumper for her lunch. I watch her sit up taller, smiling, but not at me, trying out expressions in the window at her reflection. Smiling then not. Smiling then not. And then we are drawing into the station and it goes black.

Uncle Huw would have been interested to know that a porter did help me with my trunk. The bus was waiting for us, but Phyllis didn't help me. It wasn't in a nasty way; it was because, to her, I wasn't there any more. Someone else, a boy from Greenhill I think, a boy who probably thought he was in love with Phyllis, helped her. I let her go ahead and she got on the bus. I thought, I'll just wait for the next one. I was standing on the pavement, watching, as the bus roared by. She was inside, behind the glass with the other girls in sixth-form uniform. I looked around.

There were others like me, small, in new uniforms, but they were all with each other. There wasn't anyone else alone. Oh, good, I thought. The last thing I want is to be with them.

CHAPTER 35

It's Christmas now, in London, at the end of my first term at Maldwyn Girls. Uncle Huw and Auntie Maggie are the guests, being polite, not knowing where things are kept in the kitchen. I feel sorry for them. At half-term, I'd ended up going to Janet's tall, grey house in Glasgow where her parents talked in an accent I found hard to understand. She and I had sat up all night deliberately not talking about Phyllis, who was on the French exchange, imagining a future for ourselves I still can't believe in. David seems to have got younger while he was away. He has been washed in colour and light and I have been darkened by cloud and rain and misery and sin.

'You have lost the way that things are done in England,' I tell him. He is starting to get wheezy again. I can see it happening.

Mum says, 'Don't make him laugh.' Laughing is the killer. So here we all are sitting around the table. It's about halfway through and everyone's pulled crackers and the candle flames are flickering as hats are unfurled and placed on heads and there's the smell of wine and turkey

228

fat. I've got a thimble of wine, which is going to my head, and so has Phyllis but she doesn't touch hers and she's back to pushing her food around her plate instead of eating it. Mum and Dad were shocked when they saw her at the airport, I could tell, but their technique was not to say anything, not to say that she has got thin because that is what she wants them to say. They ignore it, like they do when they think she has put on weight. The idea is to carry on as if nothing has happened. So, we are all eating our Christmas dinner and Auntie Maggie and Uncle Huw are accepting compliments on the succulence of the turkey they brought from the Finns' farm, and Mum is accepting compliments for the crispness of the roast potatoes and the smoothness of the gravy, and David is telling a joke from a cracker about why the chicken crossed the road, and we are all pulling out little sewing kits and puzzles and plastic toys that children and dogs could get stuck in their throats. Stella and Midnight are in the conservatory wondering where they are. Stella has got a bone and Midnight is sitting in a seed tray looking angrily out across London and wagging her tail. And then Dad spoils it. He makes a mistake. It makes me think how easy it is to make mistakes, this tightrope we are all treading all the time.

'Phyllis,' he says.

She looks up at him with the big brown eyes and his mouth wobbles but hers stays perfectly still and beautiful. Mum puts her hand out but he takes it and puts it back in her lap where it belongs.

'It's Christmas Day, darling,' Mum tells him.

'Exactly,' he says. We're all silent. 'It's Christmas bloody Day and she won't eat a bloody thing.' Phyllis looks at him again with the big brown eyes. Mum's fill with tears. Phyllis looks at them both, then she gets up from the table, very carefully, remembering it is Christmas bloody Day and she shouldn't make too much of a fuss. She folds up her napkin on her side plate and goes out quietly. There have been so many meals when she has left the table. We all look at Auntie Maggie. We know now that she hadn't worked such wonders in Priestmeadow; it had been Edward who had worked the wonders. I watch David help himself to more potatoes.

'Let's not spoil the meal,' Auntie Maggie says. 'She'll have a little morsel later.'

I think of Phyllis lying on her bed upstairs, of how she had lain by the grave, of the moss in her hair. There is no point in me going to her. No point in anyone going. Except Edward Furnace and he is dead. Then, after a few minutes, quite taking us by surprise, she comes back in. Her eyelids are swollen so no one says anything about the food. I collect the plates with hers on top and divide her meat between Midnight and Stella. She has a little bit of pudding, currant by raisin, and afterwards there is the Queen's speech and David and I play Mastermind Royale and *The Wizard of Oz* is on TV. I see Phyllis watching Dad out of the corner of my eye. I know she doesn't want to hurt him.

CHAPTER 36

Eira was thinking of Christmases. Of Phyllis's anorexia. She was walking with Ray. They did a lot of walking because it was easier looking outwards, not staring at each other across a table. She was trying to explain how Phyllis slipped out of her parents' control. How she could have gone to university but she hadn't and how she had even turned down a place at Oxford, which was so typical of her. She said she wanted to act and she went round old people's homes, singing songs from the nineteen forties, because you had to do a certain number of live performances to stand a chance of getting your Equity card. Eira loved those songs. The song she loved best was 'Sentimental Journey'. But Eira was still at Maldwyn Girls' College then and she only heard about Phyllis occasionally, only saw her when their paths happened to cross. No one said anything about the distance between them because it was another of those things that was not spoken of. Their parents had come back from Fiji and David started at a school in Muswell Hill. At one point, Phyllis had gone back home to live with them. At first, they were pleased when she came home. They still had illusions about how they could feed her up. She wanted to go to drama school but audition after audition went by and she didn't get in, not even to a bad one. There were sometimes phone calls Eira heard or conversations going on about whether it was the right song or the right Shakespearian soliloquy. Eira saw her in a play once but she was only good because she looked the part. She played Elvira in *Blithe Spirit*. It was a play full of young people pretending to be old people, and she was the thinnest girl by miles. Then she was admitted to hospital.

Ray didn't say Eira had a long tongue. She didn't make small replies that anyone could have made when she was with Ray. Something was changing in her. She wondered if she could tell him the truth about what happened, even though she had never told Jack. She would never tell her parents, but for some reason she felt that she might tell Ray. They were on a bus in Islington. Always on the move, travelling through the city – just the two of them together, and all the other people rushing along the pavement below. She felt so close to him after such a short time and she put her hand on his and he enclosed it with his hand. She leaned her head against his shoulder and wondered if this could be the beginning of love. She decided to take Ray to Priestmeadow.

★ ★ ★

When they arrived at Priestmeadow, they walked through the town and out the other side and into a field of buttercups, thistles and bright orange horseflies. They were sitting very close, their sides touching. That afternoon they had checked into a black-beamed inn on the outskirts of Hay-on-Wye. Then they had hurried out into the sun, into the possibility of the day. Maude was expecting them for tea, but first Eira was showing Ray around. When they walked past Auntie Maggie's and Uncle Huw's old house, she pointed out the room she had slept in as a child with the moth-eaten curtains, where now there was red and white gingham snapping in the wind. He looked at the house. To him, she thought, it is just an old stone house by a river. Roses had been planted up the front and the window-sills had been painted a fashionable slatey-blue. Eira led Ray through a gap in the fence into the spinney and down to the river where someone had made a little lake and an ornamental garden. They were trespassing. The boathouse had disappeared, but the river flowed on as before. They walked on towards Maude's house but they were too early so they kept walking and they ended up in the big wood at the foot of the ruined castle. And she found the mossy rock, near the glade with bracken growing thickly all around it. She cleared a small space in the bracken with an old branch and sat down, pulling him down after her so the bracken towered above them and they were like two nesting birds. She held his warm hand very tightly inside the bracken cave and she told him exactly what had happened, down to every last detail that she could remember. On and on without stopping, the words spilling out into the warm, dusty air. How she had made Edward run away because he thought Phyllis didn't love him. About the birth in the spinney. About the burial. The baby's bones were in the earth inside their locked box with the carved birds. All turned to dust. And Edward dying. And about being on the train and going to Maldwyn Girls' College and not being able to speak another word. Phyllis didn't know who the father was. She loved Edward but she didn't really know if the baby was his. Or Matthew's. It was like Mary Evans – she told him that story too. 'It was the death of Phyllis. It was the death of her.' On and on, her long tongue carving out the air.

'Eira,' said Ray. 'Look at me.' But she could not. 'Eira, you were ten.'

'Don't tell me life must go on as if nothing has happened,' she said.

'No. Of course not. Not as if nothing has happened. Not nothing.'

Ray took her hands and laid them on the mossy rock. 'You were a child who did not understand. I am just an ordinary man, and I don't know anything about anything, but sitting here in this wood, in this beautiful wood . . .' He held her in his arms for a long time and she sighed a deep sigh. And a butterfly flew into the air, out of her mouth, a blue butterfly, a beautiful blue butterfly the colour of a perfect summer sky.

'How did you do that?' she said.

'I don't know,' he said. 'It must have landed on your lips.' And then he kissed her.

Just for that one moment, she thought afterwards, it had seemed that they could have loved each other. That day in Priestmeadow when he had made possible what had once seemed impossible.

CHAPTER 37

The Lux baby was born. Daisy Lux did not die in childbirth and nor did the child die. Mother and baby were doing fine, said Henry. It was all fine. Eira wondered how painful it had been, but no one mentioned any pain. The child was to be called Cosima, a name Eira would never have called any child of hers, so at least that was all right. It was the one good thing. Henry Lux wore the gloss of his fatherhood handsomely. He said things which were as painful to Eira as if he had taken a sharp piece of glass and scratched them onto her face. Her face stayed smiling and pleasant. He said, until you are a parent, you have no idea about x and y and z. Until you are a parent, like me, basically, you have no idea about anything. Eira thought, it is you who have no idea about anything; it is you who do not understand.

'You have to have this actually happen to you before you understand,' he said. Eira thought, but I am not the same as you. Don't think that I am the same as you, Henry Lux.

Too soon, Daisy brought the baby through the park and into the museum. Cosima. She lay dark and pink against the white background of her old-fashioned pram that Daisy had rigged up with a lacy parasol, lest one beam of light should touch the face of her dark pink child. Daisy smiled softly. She seemed like a creature without its shell, cakey and doughy and podgy round the edges. Eira felt a terrible violence towards her. She felt murderous. She thought, No, no, no, no. Do not get your breasts out and start feeding the baby when I am here. I may dissolve. I may start crying like a baby. Daisy did not start feeding the baby then. But, Eira thought, she will. One day soon, she will and I will not know where to look or how to control myself when she does this. Daisy Lux will think that it is right that she should be able to feed her baby in the broad light of day without being made to feel a pariah. She will think that it is natural because she likes all things natural. She would expect that Eira would too, and Eira did. Very much. But it was not that, it was just that seeing it twisted her stomach so much, it made her not be able to find enough air to breathe. Eira looked and pretended to coo at the baby as society dictated she should. It was expected. This was all there was to do. It was not possible to say, 'No, go away, go away, I do not want you here. Leave me alone here in the dark museum, leave me, leave me. Leave me and take your baby away.' When Eira looked at Cosima, all she saw was a strange and ugly combination of the parents' faces, what they must have looked like as babies.

She shuddered. This baby was not a patch on the little baby she'd found, sweet little baby Fatima with the tea-coloured skin and the dark jewel eyes. Her baby. This Lux baby would never want for anything. This Lux baby would have everything planned and perfect in her life. No one would ever leave her outside a museum.

Eira peered beneath the parasol at the baby's focusless eyes and the wet, bubbling, sucking, working little mouth and said, 'She's so beautiful, she's so beautiful,' over and over again. 'She's the most beautiful baby I have ever seen.' And they thought that what she said was true. They looked at the baby too, their eyes could not leave her, and Eira kept on saying those words and murmuring those words until it was time for Daisy to leave. When they had gone, she shut herself in the cleaning cupboard and sat among the bottles of disinfectant and mops and wept. And when she came back out, she thought how big the museum was, yet how oppressive, and how she was never someone who should have been working in a museum – in such a cold, dark tomb of a place, when all she wanted was light. Anyone could see that this was wrong.

The next day, because Ray was a friend of the Luxes, he came with her to see the baby again at their house. Eira watched him and wanted to be good and kind like he was. He lifted Cosima into the air and then down and the baby loved the feeling of the air going past in a rush and she didn't cry. He did it again with his big strong arms grasping the tiny body. The baby was startled by Ray but not so much that he made her cry. Ray laughed a lot and he made a fuss of the baby but in a strong and manly way. And then he moved the conversation on to other things. And he kept his hand behind Eira's back, stroking a small piece of her skin, with his thumb where no one could see, over and over again, and he didn't talk about the baby afterwards. He just stopped her on the pavement and hugged her tight. But then his phone rang and he turned his back to answer it and wandered off a little way down the street on his own. When he came back up to her, he seemed awkward. He told her he had to go back to the recording studio, and he couldn't meet her eyes. And an image of the girl at Paddington Station came into Eira's mind. 'It's okay,' she said, 'I want to be on my own, anyway.'

When she got home, there was a message on the answer phone. She guessed what the news was because of her mother's tone of voice. It was a trembling voice. She poured herself a glass of red wine and drank it slowly, watching the sun set above the park, the sky red-raw between the black leaves of the trees. When she moved, she felt stiff, like an old person, and when she looked in the mirror, she noticed the creases at the corners of her eyes and more white hair sprouting out of her parting. 'I am old,' she said. 'How can I ever have a baby when my skin is turning into a crumpled bag and my bones are wearing thin as honey-combs?' She picked up the phone and dialled her mother's number and the news was good. The news was that Jyoti and David were going to have a baby too. This was different from the Lux baby. She did feel very happy, because it was just the right thing and this baby would be the flesh and blood of her own flesh and blood so it was different. The family needed a baby in its midst. Eira imagined her mother throwing her tapestry into the fire, emerging from the cocoon of her beige sitting room as a fully-fledged grandmother – in brightness and in health, a slick of lipstick, a new role at last. She imagined her father quickly filling in the gaps of his birds, slap dash, hurrying down the stairs, tearing off his painting shirt. She phoned David and Jyoti straight away and they were pleased and taking it in their stride and it would all be all right, she knew. They knew to be gentle with her and they tried to talk to her about this new thing she had going with Ray. When she had said goodbye, she lay down on the floor and cried and the cries came out as terrible shouts. It was the sort of crying that could have been heard on the street.

CHAPTER 38

Eira was on a plane going to Fiji. It would be landing soon. From the window she could see mangrove swamps and rainforest and turquoise waters and a line of foam, scallop-edged. She was travelling alone. No one had been there to hold her hand at take-off and no one would hold her hand when they landed, even though she was afraid of flying. No one saw her off at the airport. She felt afraid and tired and as old as her years. She was as old as her mother had been when she was flying back to England from Fiji, not knowing what had happened to her daughters that summer at Priestmeadow and never knowing. Eira would have liked to have been able to say that Ray was there, by her side, but Ray didn't want to have a baby, didn't want to settle down. It was good she had found out when she did. He wasn't ready yet, even though he was forty-three. All the men she fell in love with were like that: not ready. If they had met when they were younger, perhaps Ray could have grown into it, thinking it was just for the moment but then it would have turned into the rest of their lives.

One day, it might be different with another man. Or it might not.

So, it wasn't the happy ending she wanted it to be. Her happy ending was not in sight. Maybe there was no happy ending for her. There wasn't for Phyllis. Not after her seventeenth summer. Not for Edward. He was only a boy. On the plane there were lots of children crying, parents holding them, taking care of them. And there were the older people, who had had their children years and years ago, going to visit their grandchildren, because their families branched out like trees of singing birds. Then there were the young ones who were certain they would have children one day. It was only a matter of time for them. Last of all, there were the people like her who hadn't had children, who went through the world alone and left no trace. Not so many of them. Some didn't want children. Some couldn't have them. Some were still waiting and hoping. Some of them felt that if they couldn't have a child, they would die. She was fulfilling a childhood wish to go to Fiji. She had left her job in the museum and given up her tower. She could do things like that because she had no one to support, no one to be responsible for except herself. When she got back, she could go to an employment agency and they would find her a job. But something else might happen first. She might meet someone who would tie her to one particular part of the earth and she could look for a job near there. For now, she was taking a gap. It could be a gap year if she could find things to do to pay her way. Or it could be just a small gap before she hurried back to London. Ray was not for her after all. But he had done one thing that day in Priestmeadow. He had done the most important thing that anyone could have done, even though she couldn't exactly explain it in words. She was tired of words. She'd put a sketchbook in her case and some paints. But her paintings wouldn't be like her father's. They'd be her unique take on things. She didn't know what would happen to her now. But it didn't matter because no one knows what will happen. She had always wanted to go for a trip in a glass-bottomed boat.

The Lux baby, Cosima Lux, was all right really. She was just another human being. Eira had even held her a couple of times. When Daisy breastfed, Eira looked up at the sky or out of the window at the trees and thought about the arrival of autumn, the change of the season. It was time for her to get away from the Luxes. When David's baby was born she wouldn't be in the country. But that was all right. It just so happened she wouldn't be in the country. They didn't need her. It was between each other. They were the parents. They would send her photos in emails, and she would receive them in Internet cafés far away and when she got back she would be better equipped to be an aunt. Or perhaps she wouldn't really be better. Perhaps she would be just the same. Whenever she closed her eyes, she made sure her mind was full of the birds and butterflies and tropical fish she was hoping to see. She didn't know how long she would be able to last like this, alone. She knew she was becoming warped and stunted like a tree on some far, rocky outcrop. A tree where no birds sang. She didn't know what she would do if she did not have a child. If she couldn't. But the possibility was still just about there. Just. And the possibility was there that she would not. The plane was preparing to land now. From morn to noon they had been travelling. From noon to dewy eve. A summer's day . . . There. That was the moment of touchdown. She clasped her own hands in each other for want of any other hands. There was a bounce and then they kept on rushing along fast, as if they couldn't stop and they were going to take off again. Going fast, she thought, on and on, like we all do when we live, fast into our lives of not knowing, not knowing if we'll crash or if we'll come to a gradual stop. If only life were made of glass, the future, the square of my future, so I could see it. But we can't see. It's all unknown. That's what it is being human.

ACKNOWLEDGEMENTS

Poppy Hampson, Alison Samuel and Caroline Dawnay.

Credits

Line from *The Highwayman*, by Alfred Noyes. Thanks to the Society of Authors as the Literary Representative of the Estate of Alfred Noyes. Lines from *Birds of Fiji in Colour*, by W. J. Belcher. Lines from 'It's a Heartache' by Bonnie Tyler, used by kind permission of BMG Music Publishing Ltd, and Lojo Music. 'Don't Take All Night', words and music by Sol Marcus and Bennie Benjamin – © 1964 Chappell & Co (Renewed) – All Rights Reserved – Lyric reproduced by kind permission of Carlin Music Corp – London NW1 8BD. 'The Honeysuckle and the Bee', words by Albert H. Fitz and music by William Penn © 1901, Sol Bloom, USA Reproduced by permission of Francis Day & Hunter Ltd, London WC2H 0QY. Line from 'My Melancholy Baby', written by George Norton and Ernie

Burnett, used by permission of Shapiro, Bernstein & Co., Inc. International copyright secured. All rights reserved.